W9-AEL-059
3 1230 00 48 9254

Bob the Gambler

BOOKS BY
FREDERICK BARTHELME

♠ ♠ ♠

MOON DELUXE

SECOND MARRIAGE

TRACER

CHROMA

TWO AGAINST ONE

NATURAL SELECTION

THE BROTHERS

PAINTED DESERT

BOB THE GAMBLER

Bob the Gambler

FREDERICK
BARTHELME

HOUGHTON MIFFLIN COMPANY
BOSTON • NEW YORK
1997

Library of Congress Cataloging-in-Publication Data
Barthelme, Frederick, date.
Bob the gambler / Frederick Barthelme.
p. cm.
ISBN 0-395-80977-0
I. Title.
PS3552.A763B63 1997
813'.54 — dc21 97-4363 CIP

Printed in the United States of America

Book design by Robert Overholtzer

QUM 10 9 8 7 6 5 4 3 2 1

For Dawn

Bob the Gambler

What I'd always liked about Biloxi was the decay, the things falling apart, the crap along the beach, the skeletons of abandoned hotels, the trashy warehouses and the rundown piers jutting out into the dirty water, so I wasn't thrilled that in the last five years our dinky coast town had been turned into an outlet-mall version of Las Vegas, with a dozen cartoon casinos, lots of gussied-up Motel 6 hotel rooms, an ocean of slicked-back hair, and a big increase in unsavory tourists. We'd had plenty of unsavory tourists before the casinos. Anyway, it was August, and things were way past steamy, and I guess Jewel and I were doing O.K., but I didn't have any architectural work so we were living on savings and her income, which was enough to get by, but not more. On Sunday, after the NFL preseason game, there wasn't anything to do, and we were sitting on the porch quiet as mice when she held up the newspaper and said, "Raymond. Let's go here and do this," and *here* was the Paradise casino, a dozen blocks away on the beach in Biloxi, and *this* was gambling.

I'd been to Vegas on the standard teenager-leaves-home trip

when I was eighteen, playing slots, craps, getting a close-up look at a real prostitute, the rest of that, so I wasn't dying to see the inside of a casino, although I guess I was curious about adult gambling, like the kind you did when you had a bank account. Still, I resisted the invitation.

"I don't think so," I said.

The porch was a glassed-in room at the back of our renovated three-bedroom wood-siding bungalow, looking out at a small back yard rimmed in crepe myrtles, most of which we'd planted ourselves half a dozen years before because we liked the blooms and the body-builder skin. Jewel shoveled me the *Sun-Herald* and nicked it with a fingernail to point out the place-mat-size photo above the fold, printed in gaudy out-of-register color. The Paradise.

I crimped the paper for a better look at a chart that used gold coins to show how much money the casinos were making on the Mississippi coast.

"We can blaze a trail through the night sky and all that," she said. "That's what you promised."

"I was trying to seduce you," I said. "Besides, that was fifty years ago." I held up the paper. "It says they're getting us for two billion a year."

"Maybe they are," she said. "But that doesn't mean *I* won't win."

"What, you got a magic wand?" I went back to the paper, hoping she'd forget it.

"We roll," Jewel said, getting out of her chair.

"Wait a minute. What about RV? Is she around?"

RV was our daughter, Jewel's daughter, fourteen years old, by Jewel's first husband, Mr. Clark Festival, whom she married for a year, fifteen years before. According to Jewel, he was just a rat. We were lucky he hadn't been seen in years.

"RV's over at Mallory's raging against the machine. Either

that or raging against curfews, injustice, food additives, Aerosmith, allowances, stuff like that, only they do it alphabetically, I believe."

"I don't think it's nice of you to make fun of your own daughter."

"Not making fun," Jewel said. "Anyway, she won't be home until late. There's a church function." Jewel was moving, collecting papers, stacking them on the three-legged coffee table. "What about, it's my money and I'll gamble if I want to?"

"Not wife-like," I said. "You're a big help."

Jewel covered her face in mock contrition. "I couldn't resist. I'm sorry. C'mon, you can go. We should've been by now."

She came over and tugged at my arm. The dog Frank eyed her from his corner of the porch. He was sixty pounds and brown, something short of clean in the blood.

"I could take coat hangers to the laundry," I said. "They still pay two cents apiece for coat hangers?" Some buds from the crepe myrtles close to the house were bleeding down the porch glass. I dumped the entertainment section on her stack.

"Was a joke, McGee," she said.

"Do I have to get dressed? Oh, no, I remember. They go in their underpants. What about shoes? Do I have to wear shoes?"

"Step on a nail and we have to get shots."

"Yes on shoes," I said.

She was wearing some retro shirt with black shoulders and checks below, open over a T-shirt and black jeans so tight around her ankles that it was hard to imagine how she'd gotten her feet through. She was thinner than she'd been in years. This was exciting to me, but I pretended it wasn't.

"How'd you get into those?" I asked, pointing to the narrow pants.

"Never mind," she said.

She wouldn't eat. She served herself full meals, or ordered

big if we were out, then pushed the food around on her plate in a merry-go-round of vegetables and entrée.

"Are you depressed about something?" I said.

"Not me. I'm Happy Girl. We're going to the Paradise casino to have fun. I'm thinking we don't have one single problem. I'm happy with you, RV, work, the house, and the brown dog Frank."

"You got stick legs," I said.

"I saw the doctor for you," she said. "He said I was fine. All he did was unbutton my blouse and admire me. The all-important breast exam, his favorite."

"You told me," I said. "I offered to go beat him up."

"I'm your baby."

"You got that lean and bony look," I said.

"Well, a lot of men like the look." She did a runway-model turn. "Perfect for my moment in history. You, on the other hand, are as fat as a party balloon. But hey, Ray, you don't have to go see no doctor. I'm here, fat or not. I earn the money, cook the food, clean the house, cater to your prepubescent fantasies."

"Hear you roar," I said, flicking off the porch light I'd noticed earlier. It had been on since the night before.

"So go change," she said.

She let Frank out while I went into the bedroom looking for a real shirt. Then we locked up the house, chose her Ford Explorer over mine, and headedggg for the beach.

The Paradise was a floating warehouse. It was six shades of purple, trimmed in violet and lime, slathered with neon and row lights. Thirty-foot playing cards ran up its side. The whole building was washed in pink light that swaggered back and forth. It was forty-five feet from land, anchored by pilings thirty feet in diameter, four to a side. A narrow moat separated the casino from the parking lot on one side and from the drive-up entrance along its length in front. The casino had to float, that was the ordinance, but the city had a convenient idea of what floating was. Where the Paradise connected to the land there were huge steel knuckle joints, like zippers with teeth the size of tires.

Like all surviving casinos, the Paradise was good for the economy — a six-acre parking garage, a thirty-eight-floor hotel, two auditoriums, a half-dozen restaurants and clubs, a couple of kids' centers, a mini-arcade of specialty shops, and God knows what else. A lot of jobs building it, running it, maintaining it.

The building was everything an architect wouldn't do, an eyesore — turrets, exposed steel, corrugated-metal siding, garish colors, an unending supply of neon and glass — a joke on itself, but the kind of joke you got used to, like when somebody put a twenty-foot fish on the front of a restaurant. One day you gave the fish a name, then your wife or your kid picked it up, and pretty soon the restaurant was a landmark, and you'd say, "Hey, Needlenose," every time you drove by.

Inside, everything binged and wizzled, everything was fast, especially sound. It was like a monster video arcade souped up with time-lapse photography and on Fast Forward with a thousand chrome machines cheek by jowl, each occupied by a big butt stuffed in blue jeans, an old woman with a bent cigarette dripping out of her wizened face, a muscle guy with babes on both knees, a drunk college kid, a biker, a cowgirl, or some other human being. The machines were like running off at the mouth, popping and dinging.

"Hey, it's Tokyo," I said.

"Yeah, like when Tokyo's cool and futuristic. We're supposed to be amazed."

"I am, I am."

The carpet was spongy, thick, patterned some ridiculous

black-and-red wavy way. We stood in a raised area by the doors next to a security guard in purple pants and a white shirt. His name tag said "Petrie." He carried a gold-plated pistol buckled into a holster that had a head of Christ ringed in stars tooled into the leather. People scooted around, there was lots of shouting, waitresses roamed, dealers in white shirts, black pants, and satiny red bow ties stood behind player-jammed tables planted back-to-back. Guys looking swarthy and slightly menacing stood around in big handsome suits, every hair in place, watching the action. The gamblers were forlorn, or giddy. They dressed down, moved as if lost. Seemed worried. Skittered back and forth between machines and tables, smacking each other on the back, giving each other high-fives, blistering the room with shouts and gestures.

I was surprised how much the excess appealed to me. I said, "You sure this is where we want to be?"

"That's a big yes," she said, snapping my arm, pulling me down the steps. "It's fine. We'll lose our money and then we'll have dinner and go home."

"Great," I said, reaching for my wallet. "I'll start the money now." I tossed a twenty on the floor. A passing waitress stopped and picked up the bill, handed it back to me, laughing politely.

"See, they even like your jokes," Jewel said.

We didn't lose. Jewel hit a jackpot on a Wild Cherry slot and was two hundred dollars ahead. She played quarters at first, then moved up to dollars. That was great, especially when she won. After a time I wandered off to check out the Slot Salon, where the five-, ten-, and twenty-five-dollar machines lived. I had gotten a couple of hundred-dollar bills, and tried one on a Sizzlin' 7 machine. It paid, then took back what it had paid. I was putting the second hundred into a five-dollar Double Diamond when Jewel walked up with tubs full of dollar tokens. The machine spit my hundred back out.

"I'm up four. What about you?" she said.

"Four hundred?"

She nodded, holding up the quart cups of tokens she was carrying. "I've got to cash out. These are way too heavy. You playing this five-dollar?"

"Yeah, but I'd rather play the hundred." I jerked my head toward a short row of hundred-dollar slot machines behind us. "I could use your money. That'd be four shots."

"No way," she said. "Get your own." She brushed her hair back out of her face, balancing the Paradise cups against her chest. "What do they pay, anyway?"

"Sixteen thousand, thirty-two. Three red sevens is a hundred thousand."

"Oh, like we're really hitting that."

"Hey, you're the gambler," I said. "Get that money changed."

"Forget it," she said.

"So try it here." I tapped the five-dollar machine.

"Don't like it." She took her cups and left.

I stuck my hundred into the machine again. A couple of times, until the machine finally bit. I hit Credits so I'd get twenty credits, not coins dumped into the tray. The coins made a racket when they dropped. I punched Play One Coin, then Spin. Nothing. I did that again, and a third time. The woman next to me said, "You ought to be playing two, in case you hit the jack." She thumped the glass above my reel windows, where the payoffs were backlit.

"Oh yeah?" The payoffs were straight doubles except for the triple double-diamond jackpot. "It's double for everything but the big one."

"Don't do it then," she said, flicking her hand at me as she thumbed her Play Two Coins button. Some of the machines took two coins, some three. "You'll be sorry. This is experience talking. I did it once."

"Hit the jackpot?"

"Yeah, this one right here," she said, nodding at the slot in front of her. "Three months ago. Three double diamonds with one coin. It was five grand, but if I'd had two coins —"

"You'd be a wealthy woman today."

She gave me aren't-you-cute. "I wouldn't have lost it all that night," she said. She was in her forties, gray hair, scraggly clothes, a purse the size of a saucepan. She smoked nonstop and her cigarettes had big rosy flowers on their filter tips. She had scads of blue eye shadow. For all that, she wasn't ugly. "You been playing long?"

"First time here," I said. "My wife — that was her a minute ago — she won on the dollars. She's cashing in to play these."

"That ain't what I heard," the woman said.

"Well, I don't know. How about you?"

"I play all the livelong day," she said. "I play until I can't stand up anymore, and until I can't sit down. Then I go home and sleep awhile. I've been doing it since they got here. But only this casino. It's my favorite. I like the people. I win here. Well, win as much as I lose. You stay after it and that's what happens. If you play and run, you're dead meat, you're leaving a loser. That's what happened to me and my husband, Beau. Before he died, anyway."

"I'm sorry about that."

"Ah, that was last year. He died right here in the casino. Wouldn't have had it any other way." She pointed toward the table games. "He was at a craps table out yonder and just keeled over. Heart attack. Worst night of my life, I guess. After that I started coming solo, and then I met somebody new, and we got married, so it all worked out. He's a wonderful guy. He's in auto cleaning and detailing, got a place out on Woodman Road."

She had three hundred credits — fifteen hundred dollars — in the machine. "You ahead all that?"

She looked at her counter. "Yeah, most of it. I think I'm in a couple hundred, about."

"That's great. I'd take a rest if I had it."

"Yeah, you and every other coon hound on the block." She looked around and waved at nobody in particular. "They tell you to go every time you win a nickel. They really love you here. They take your money, but they love you while they're doing it."

They looked mostly twenty-five or thirty, healthy, like people who work the malls. Ruddy-faced or plain or squirrelly-haired — you couldn't tell one from the next. The uniforms didn't help. Tux shirts for everybody. Little aprons for some. A few of the dealers were older, a few cocktail people looked shopworn. The woman sitting next to me started up again.

"See, they feel guilty. They watch us lose and this builds a reservoir of affection, so they want us to win. It won't hurt them. They have jobs, salaries, tips. The older ones come from Atlantic City, or Vegas. The floor and shift people get juiced in, you know, from other places they've worked, but dealers, pits, waitresses, they're all pretty much local. They make six an hour."

"Jesus." I punched the Play One Coin button, this lighted green square the size of a matchbook on the front of my machine. "That's not so much, is it?"

"I don't know. Tips run high. Winners go tip-happy. My daughter waitresses at the Palace. She's cut seven hundred dollars in one night."

"No kidding?" I punched the Spin button. "I'd waitress for that kind of money."

"That's it," the woman said. "I carry some waitress time myself. Got a problem with my hands now, though."

A huge burly guy came up. He had a three-day growth of beard and dirty brown hair that sat on his head like an order of chili. His sweatshirt said "America the Beautiful." He put his arms around the woman, kissed her ear. "How's Baby?" he said.

"Baby be fine," she said. "This fellow here wants to be a waitress."

The giant looked none too friendly.

"We were kidding around," I said. "She was talking about her daughter — her daughter's a waitress, you know."

"Hey, I know that," the guy said, smiling too big for me.

"Uh-huh." I tried to think of something else to say, some way to get out. "So, well, congratulations to the both of you."

The guy got me on the shoulder. "You winning or losing?" he said.

"Losing." He was thumbing my collarbone.

"You know, I never would have guessed that. You look so much like a winner." He was a toothy guy. He stuck out a hand the size of a baseball glove. "My name's Winky Cohen," he said. "This is my wife, Baby."

I shook his hand. "How are you?" I said. "Ray Kaiser." I smiled at Baby and then turned around to look for Jewel. "Maybe I'll win when my wife gets back with our money."

"*Their* money," Baby said. "You hear that, Winky?" The new husband nuzzled her ear some more, sat down at the machine next to hers, grabbed some coins from her tray, started poking them into the machine.

I craned my neck and swiveled my chair looking for Jewel. "Wonder where she is. Maybe I'll go find her. She's at the main cage, that's over here, right?"

Baby pointed to her left without turning around, without missing a beat on her machine. The reels came up — double bar, double bar, double diamond. She slapped the machine on its chrome face and squealed, then high-fived the big guy. He squealed just like her.

"Hey! Way to hit," I said, looping a high-five toward the woman, missing her palm and catching part of her wrist, twisting her arm. She yelped.

"Damn, I'm sorry."

"Baby all right?" Winky said, bending around in front of her.

"Fine," she said, giving me a look.

"What's that worth?" He was looking at the reels, then at the payout chart above.

"Thousand," the woman said.

"Ha! We're running with the big dogs now," he said.

Jewel was in the dollar slots with five hundred credits and a tray of tokens. I took the chair beside her and said, "What's going on? I've been looking for you thirty minutes."

"Bullshit. You've been eyeing the babes," she said. The blinking lights above us were reflected in her eyes.

"They're one-nighters, for sure," I said. "I thought you were cashing out."

"No way. I hit it again, a couple more times. This machine is paying everything. I'm here forever."

She looked frazzled, excited. Her hair was bent and there were creases in her makeup and her shirt was out and wrinkled. We'd been at the casino only a couple of hours. I touched her forearm as she was punching the Play Three Coins button. "Hey," I said.

"Hey what? What?"

"Take it easy. You want a break? You've got the big win already."

"Don't be messing with my arm," Jewel said. "There's plenty more in here, and I haven't even started with the quantum mechanics. I was talking to a guy on this bank of machines over here." She pointed to her left, over the top of the machine she was on, at some machines on the other side. "There's a guy over there, anyway, he was telling me how quantum mechanics works and how you can make the symbols come up the way you want. You think hard how you want them and that reorganizes the atoms. And there's something else — quantum mechanics and something else, I forget what."

I put my forehead down on the face of the machine next to hers. The chrome was mighty cool, but when I opened my eyes I got this closeup of greasy fingerprints. I lifted my head.

"Morphic resonance," she said. "That's like you're standing there and you feel somebody staring at you, and you turn around and somebody *is.* And you knew it before you looked. Morphic resonance."

"I got it. What if I don't feel the bars coming up together? What do I do then?"

"Jesus, ever since you sat down I'm losing. You're bad karma or something," Jewel said.

"Maybe I'll go stare at some other people," I said.

"I don't know, he was just telling me about it. It was working for him. He kept hitting sevens. Hit 'em six times in a row. I don't know what he was using. But I don't need to use either one, the way this guy's hitting, the way it was hitting before you got here. I can punch this baby till I drop. All night long. I don't think it'll ever stop paying." Then she hit three single bars. The machine started dinging and raised her credits. She got a hand on my shoulder, pushing me away. "See?"

I watched her hit the triple-coin button another half-dozen times. When nothing came up she had a crisis of faith, fast. I had to take a walk for her. When I returned she had fallen back against her chair, her arms by her sides, flopping loosely. She slumped. Her credits were down to two hundred eighty.

"Fuck this," she said. "This machine is fucked."

"I wasn't here or even thinking of being here," I said. "Cash out, and I'll buy you dinner. I'll buy you a hamburger."

"God, a whole one?" she said. "You didn't win anything?"

"Nope." I reached across her and punched the Cash button. Coins started splashing into the tray. They came fast at first, then more slowly, erratically, the machine sounding as if it were stirring coins. Then it stopped altogether, a hundred seventy coins short. The light on top of the machine started blinking.

"What's with this?"

"Needs a fill," she said. "It happened a minute ago."

A four-foot woman in a blue stretch outfit came up, pulled a long zoot-suit chain out of her pocket, and stuck the key into the side of the machine. "Excuse me," she said, shooing us out of the way. She opened the face of the machine and looked inside, then took her walkie-talkie and read "eight-oh-two" off the side of the machine. "You're doing pretty well, huh?" she said to Jewel.

Jewel was sweeping coins out of the tray and plugging them into the next machine, punching the button. "Well, I was doing pretty well until my husband came up and put the kibosh on the deal. And this is my first time."

"First time?" the woman said. "Where're you from?"

"Oh, we live here, we just never came to the casino before," Jewel said. "He's a late adopter."

I smiled at the mini-woman, thinking how strange she was. I couldn't take my eyes off her. She wasn't out of proportion or anything, just small. Stuck with it. She probably had extensions on the pedals in her car, that kind of thing. There was something about her face, it looked like a Halloween mask, the skin did. One of those rubber jobs. She had an odd scar across the bridge of her nose, running down along the left nostril.

"Well, get out while you're ahead, that's what I say." She looked off toward the center of the casino. "They'll be here in a minute with your fill."

I scooped coins out of the tray and dropped them into a quart bucket with the Paradise logo printed on its side. "We're cashing in."

Jewel scrambled for coins. She was trying to get them before I did. The woman watched for a minute, then said, "Looks to me like you two lovebirds need to take a knee."

I got a quart bucket filled with dollar tokens and pointed to the cashier. "I'm changing this. You want to eat or not?"

"In a minute." Jewel was working the new machine, but it was eating her money like chocolates. "Oh, shit. O.K. You wait for the money, and I'll straighten up." She looked down at her fingers, which were newsprint black with dirt off the tokens. "I'm a mess, aren't I?"

"You're a bona fide jackpot winner," I said.

"Hey, that's better than nothing."

RV had been to a church dance with her friend Mallory. When she got home at ten-thirty, we were at the dining room table with Jewel's profits. She'd won eleven hundred dollars.

"What's all that?" RV said, sneering at the stack of hundreds.

"New money," Jewel said. "You want to touch it?"

"No, I do not want to touch it," RV said. "What's it for?"

"I won it," Jewel said.

"You went gambling?" RV was thin, too tall for her age, dark hair and big eyes. Far too pretty to be lucky. If her father was a louse, he must have been a dashing louse.

"You have fun?" I asked.

"I don't know." RV crumpled into the couch, flipped the

remote until she got MTV. The dog Frank jumped on the couch with her and she smothered him, wrapping her arm around his neck and laying her head against his. His eyes kept flicking at her, then at us, then back at RV. He looked apprehensive. She was fiddling with one of his paws, fingering his toenails. His leg jerked.

"We're using this cash here to get you a present tomorrow," Jewel said.

"Great," RV said. "I need a present. What?"

"We don't know. What do you want?"

"Car."

"Can't have a car," I said. "What's next?"

"A boyfriend," she said.

"You're only about ten years old. What do you want with a boyfriend?"

"Am not. And everybody else has a boyfriend."

"Who?" Jewel said. "Who has a boyfriend?"

"Lily," she said.

Lily was one of her two best friends, a plump, schoolmarmish tenth-grader.

"They only love her for her homework," I said.

Jewel gave me a glance, shook her head. "That is not true. They like her because she's a nice girl."

"I wish she'd do *my* homework," RV said.

Frank slithered out from under her, stepped onto the living room rug, stretched, shook, walked across the rug and onto the bare floor, his toenails clicking. He stood beside my chair.

"You want to look at the money?" I said, talking to Frank.

He put his muzzle in my lap. I scratched his ears, and whenever I started to slow down, he snapped his eyes up, the same way he'd been doing with RV. A dog threat.

"Your mother made me do it," I said. "I wanted to stay home and wait for you by the door, but she made me go to the Paradise."

"Could you please just be quiet over there?" RV said, waving at me.

Jewel scooped up the money and stuffed it into her wallet. "I think I need some private time."

She went to bathe.

I changed the sheets on our bed, thinking the Paradise was O.K., fine. Maybe they all were. Maybe they would decay, too, after a while. And the guys looking over everybody's shoulders would fall over dead and be replaced by seedy locals. That'd be an improvement. At least the locals wouldn't go for the *Scarface* look. I was glad we'd gone, glad we'd won, glad it was over.

I took Frank outside and looked at the stars. They were all there. I listened to Frank pad around the yard and wondered how I could record that. His paws on the grass, his breathing, his weaving through bushes. A great tune.

When I went in, Jewel was already in bed. RV was watching television. I kissed her goodnight and went into the bedroom. The new sheets were crisp and fresh. Jewel hadn't noticed. She was still excited about her success.

"I never thought it was that easy," she said.

"Me neither," I said.

Frank ticktacked in and threw himself down in the doorway. Sometimes he slept there, sometimes in bed with us. Mostly he slept with RV.

"Did you think it was going to be that easy? I thought we would go in there and lose all our money and that would be it," she said.

"That probably happens a lot."

"It'd be great if you could go in every once in a while and win five hundred, a thousand. That would be great."

"Yep." I pulled the sheet up under my nose and smelled the Tide. "You know, Procter and Gamble ought to market this as a perfume."

"What?" she said.

"Tide," I said. "The way these sheets smell."

"What if I told you it wasn't Tide. What if I told you it was Oxydol?"

"Well, since I washed them and put them on the bed, I'd know you were lying." I turned on my side and put an arm across her chest and rested my cheek on her bare shoulder. "Of course, we could market you as a scent. Call it Winner."

"You're a man with a lot of ideas," she said.

"You're a gambling girl," I said.

RV was three when Jewel and I first got together. We moved a lot, lived in tiny apartments, halves of houses, then moved in with her sister in Houston. I got a degree in architecture, took the exam in Texas for my license. Jewel finished a B.A. and worked as a substitute teacher. Then her sister got caught in a freak car accident on a Houston freeway — a guy ahead of her committed suicide with a shotgun at seventy miles an hour, causing a six-car collision in which Jewel's sister was two-thirds decapitated. Shortly after that we left Houston. This was the mid-eighties, years before the casinos. The coast was broken down and sloppy, a junky place to live, but we liked that. Things were simple, easy, cheap. RV was too quick and edgy for Mississippi, but when she started school she made friends readily. The schools were horrifying, but not worse than schools in Houston or anywhere else, just horrifying in different ways.

In the twenties and thirties Biloxi had been a resort, but the wind was long out of that, and in the eighties it was a runt town nobody had any use for, and that made it a relief after Houston, after everybody from Michigan moved down all at once. Those people were animals taking over the zoo. They were so happy to get out alive, I guess.

Biloxi's draw was a kind of sad-sack beach recreation — miniature golf with giant gorillas, water slides, stinky fast-food restaurants, all-night donut shops, Quik Marts, floating tricycles you pedaled in two feet of murky water off the beach, balloon rides, pontoon mini-boat rentals, stadium-size shell shops, people selling orchids, or baskets, or produce, or bathing suits out of the trunks of cars. The oldest hotels were still around then, falling down elaborately, really just husks of buildings with broken windows and rusting steel balconies overlooking the water. A few, like Captain's Crown and the Royal D'Iberville, still operated, and there you could get a room any day, any time.

The coast feeling was let it go, do it tomorrow, who cares?, what's on TV? No pressure, nowhere to go, nothing required. It reminded me of Galveston, where my father and grandparents had lived.

I got a couple of jobs with local architects, met some people, set up a small practice of my own, which did well for a time. Then, the more work I did, the more aggressive I got about being the cool designer in town and having things done my way, a legacy from my father, who was a retired lumberman living in Houston with my mother, Leona. I talked to my parents on the phone all the time when we first moved. Eight years later my mother moved over here and left my father in Houston. After that I talked to him on the phone even more. He was a sad old guy, messy, couldn't figure out why everybody had dumped him. I felt bad about that, guilty, but he *was* a hard case.

I got this local reputation as a brilliant but hard-to-get-along-with architect, which meant I got a three-page spread in *Coast* magazine, with photos of a couple of my houses, and that

I was invited to, but not expected to attend, various civic and charitable events. It also meant that the work tailed off quick. Jewel was teaching, doing PR and promotion, consulting for marketing outfits, making good enough money, so together we had more than we needed. We bought a house a few blocks off the beach in Biloxi, three bedrooms and two baths, built in the twenties, with wood siding and a dilapidated porch in back, and did a small renovation, bringing the kitchen and baths up to standard, rewiring, reframing some of the windows, glazing the porch. There was no view, though the salty Gulf smell was always around. We lived easy, walking, going for Chinese, catching movies on Saturday afternoons.

The coast was the state's big population center, seven communities strung along the Mississippi Sound, starting at Waveland and Bay St. Louis on the west, moving through Pass Christian, Long Beach, Gulfport, Biloxi, and Ocean Springs on the east, with a couple other tiny municipalities tucked in along the way. For practical purposes, it was one town with seven shopping centers and a census around three hundred thousand. Biloxi had a downtown, some businesses, a city hall, a few restaurants, and its quota of beach crap. The houses were prettier than most. They'd been built from the turn of the century through the forties by people who could afford in those days to build decent houses. Weather was balmy, or ruffled, or stormy, except in summers, when it was blazing hot, but not as bad as Texas, and we were blessed with the wonderful miracle of air conditioning. So we were O.K.

When the casinos showed, nobody knew whether they'd last, whether they'd be paddle wheelers or palaces. Mississippi didn't seem like ideal ground for a gambling industry. There were too many religious maniacs and too much fear of mobsters, thugs, thieves, the spiraling crime rate, the eradication of the genteel Southern culture, so much of which soaked the coast, right in there with the crane-size apes at Goofy Golf and Big Kahuna at Water World, and there were fierce debates, but eventually the boats came, nothing happened, the sky did not fall. All the shoddy coastal property was bought up, buildings were razed and replaced, and the new coast emerged. For most people the price was an increase in fifty-buck robberies at the convenience stores.

So we watched the coast change from a charmingly decayed backwater to a glitzy, blinking, garishly dressed highway town full of people from Miami, Chicago, Denver, from all over, come to pretend they were gamblers. By then we were locals, with a routine and a way of doing things that didn't involve the casinos at all, at least not until that Sunday in August when we went to the Paradise and won.

The first Friday night in September RV came in stumbling drunk and sick after a party. I had a scene in the yard with the goofball eighteen-year-old who drove her home, and then RV spent two hours draped over the toilet, barfing and flushing. This was a lot of fun for all of us, and we were all in there with her, rubbing her back, talking to her, passing the towels. Even the dog Frank thought it was interesting, since he always drank out of the toilet. Once RV was finished and had gone to sleep, Jewel and I swapped ideas about how we'd screwed up. When we talked to RV the next day, she told us she wasn't drinking that much, that her friends drank more than she did, that they'd been doing shots of Everclear at this guy's apartment. He was a freshman at the local junior college. The whole thing caught us by surprise — we had figured it for later, maybe sixteen.

"So why are you drinking?" Jewel said. This was the next evening.

"I don't know," RV said, doing every exasperated gesture she could think of, and that was close to a dozen. "I don't even like the taste of it. I didn't think it would have that much effect.

Lily and Mallory drank way more than me, and they didn't have a problem."

Not quite true. Jewel talked to Mallory's mother, who had found Mallory passed out on the front lawn and had taken her to the emergency room to get her stomach pumped. "You want to rethink that?" Jewel said.

"Yeah, well, maybe later. But at the party she was fine."

"So how much of this is going on?" I said.

"I don't know. Leave me alone, will you? I'm just a kid. I hated being drunk, too, you know. I'm never touching that stuff again."

We didn't get answers, so RV was grounded for a week, during which time she was sweet as could be, and we were reminded how much we liked her. Then the grounding was over and she was mobile again, running with her friends.

That lasted for another week.

Then we stopped at the drugstore one evening to get a prescription filled and ran into a group of kids in the lot, standing around the bed of a pickup. One was RV. She tried to duck, but Jewel was too quick, found her, and asked her what she was doing.

"I'm not doing anything," RV said. "I'm hanging."

"Maybe you better hang with us," Jewel said.

"Oh, Mom," RV said.

Jewel said, "Come here a minute," and motioned to RV. Something was up. You could tell. Jewel had this FBI look on her face. "Now, please."

RV swatted her hands by her sides, shrugged her shoulders, dodged her head, did everything but walk across the blacktop to where Jewel was.

"RV," Jewel said, pointing at the ground in front of her. This bothered me. It was as if she were calling a dog.

I said, "Hey, RV. Come talk to us."

There was more shrugging and dodging and weaving and gradually RV made it within ten feet of her mother. I was just watching.

"Kiss me," Jewel said.

"What?" RV said. She turned around and looked at her friends and shrugged at them as if her mother were acting crazy. She stood there in one of the exaggerated slouches that kids favor when faced with parents in public settings.

"Kiss me here," Jewel said, tapping her lips with her finger.

"Like, sure," RV said. "God, you're so embarrassing." She waved at her mother and started back toward her buddies.

I took a step as if to intercept her.

"What are *you* doing, Ray?" RV said.

I looked at Jewel, back to RV. "Enforcer?"

Jewel shook her head. "RV, come back here *now*."

RV flapped her arms and sat down square on her butt on the asphalt. "I'm not coming anywhere," she said. "I'm not going anywhere. I don't know what you people are doing."

Jewel motioned for me to get in front of RV, and Jewel came up behind, picking up RV under the arms. "Come on, dear. We'll go to the car. We're going home."

"My Walkman," RV said. "I've got all my tapes over there."

"We'll get them another day," Jewel said.

The kids by the truck were minding their own business, talking among themselves, keeping a wary eye out for what was happening to RV. One of the girls piped up and said, "Beep me later," and gave RV a wave.

I got in the back seat of the Explorer, and Jewel and RV got in front. We headed home. Jewel caught my eye in the rearview and said, "I think we've been drinking."

"I figured that out."

"Have not," RV said.

"Then why wouldn't you kiss me?"

"Oh, Mom, come on. You're so wonky sometimes."

"She's got you there," I said. "You are kind of wonky."

"You just want me to be some kind of stupid good girl all the time," RV said.

Jewel nodded, slipping into the center lane on the overpass, gliding by a Cadillac. "Yeah, I guess that's right. It's a terrible thing."

"You know what I mean," RV said.

"How much have you had to drink?" I said.

"Nothing. Not really. Part of a beer, maybe," RV said. "One beer. Maybe one and a swallow."

"Seems like more than that," Jewel said.

"Not," RV said.

"O.K.," Jewel said.

"Just leave me alone, will you," RV said.

"I can't leave you alone," Jewel said. "You're my daughter. I love you. I'm taking care of you. I don't want you out here drinking in parking lots. You're only fourteen."

"I'm almost fifteen," RV said.

"You're five months from fifteen," Jewel said.

"Four," RV said. "That's more than halfway."

Things were quiet for a minute in the car, then RV delivered a huge belch. She looked at her mother and then over her shoulder at me, as if the belch were something she was proud of, a really good joke.

I sucked some air and did a small belch myself.

"Raymond," Jewel said. "Come on."

"Sorry," I said, moving my hand at her, trying to catch her in the rearview.

"It's hard to be serious when you're burping back there," Jewel said, looking up at me.

"Right." I put my hands around the headrest of RV's seat and grabbed her neck and pretended to strangle her. "You'd better behave or we'll break your neck. Throw you in the river."

She twisted to get away from my hands. "Oh, be quiet," she said. "Leave me alone. Don't you touch me anymore."

I slid back into my seat and sighed out loud. "O.K. I won't. I am not your parent. Remember when you told me that?"

"I want a pizza," RV said, ignoring me. "No — burritos. Can we stop at Taco Bell?"

We made it through the drive-up at Taco Bell and got RV what she wanted. I ordered a half-dozen tacos, I don't know what I was thinking about. Maybe a taco party, all three of us. When we got home, Frank was at the door with one of Jewel's new cowboy boots in tow.

RV play-kicked him out of the way and went to her room, taking her burritos with her. Jewel took her boot from the dog and scolded him with a finger. "Frank, please. This is one of my boots. See?" She held up the boot and pointed at it. "Goes on my foot." She pointed at her foot. Frank was enthralled.

I put the tacos on the dining table and went into the kitchen to get a diet drink. When I got back, Jewel was sitting in her chair at the table, nibbling on the innards of a taco.

"Aren't you afraid the burrito will make her sick?" I said. There was a fly or something buzzing between the window glass and the screen. I couldn't see it, but I heard it.

"I live in hope," Jewel said.

"So, what are we doing this time?" I said. "It's not that bad, really. It's not like the last time."

"Yeah. Might have been worse if we hadn't run into her."

"Yeah, I guess," I said. "This going to her room and shutting the door — isn't there something wrong with that?"

"Kids do it. We can't force her to stay out here. She needs her privacy." Jewel was examining a chunk of ground beef she had between her fingers, held up to the light.

"I'm wondering if our relationship, mine and hers, is as good as I thought," I said. "I'm thinking, no."

"It's fine," Jewel said. "Eat your taco. Why did you get so many?" She shoved the one she'd been picking at across the table. The tissue-paper wrap made a hissing sound as it slid. I picked up her taco and bit off its end.

"Loaves and fishes," I said.

RV slammed out of her room and stomped into the kitchen. "Have we got any noodles?"

"You're having burritos and noodles?" I said.

"Come here a minute," Jewel said.

"Mom, leave me alone. I don't want to come there a minute. I want some noodles."

"Come sit down," Jewel said. "I want to talk to you."

"Oh, God." RV came back from the kitchen doing her Frankenstein walk. "Here I come. Dead girl walking."

"Sit," Jewel said, pointing to the empty chair at the end of the table.

RV wagged her head back and forth and pulled the chair out, sat on its edge facing the kitchen. Slapped her feet on the wood floor. "What?" she said.

"We've talked about this," Jewel said. "Running around, hanging out in parking lots, drinking, driving. You're fourteen. There's no point in this."

"Mom. I don't drink that much. I told you I don't even like to."

"But you do, don't you?" Jewel said.

"Well, I'm depressed. Everything's gone against me."

"Like what?"

"Everything. I'm ugly and I'm dumb and no boy even looks at me."

"You're great," Jewel said. "You're pretty and funny. What are you talking about?"

"Yeah, sure," RV said. "That's around here. But I'm different out there. I'm raging inside."

"What about?" I said.

"I don't know," RV said. "Leave me alone. I don't know."

"Are you drinking because everybody else is?" Jewel said.

"Yeah, Mom," RV said. "Sure. And if they jumped off a building, I'd jump off a building."

Frank clicked his way across the room on the hardwood floor, and RV boxed his head with her feet, banging her socks into his neck. He didn't seem to mind.

"You're going to have to be grounded again," Jewel said.

"Duh," RV said, putting all of her attention on the dog. "Like I didn't know that? Why not make it a year this time? For all the difference it'll make."

"Two weeks," Jewel said. "No phone, nothing. O.K.?"

"Sure, why not?" RV said, talking to Frank. "Who cares, anyway? I'm just a stupid kid who doesn't know anything."

"Self-esteem issues," I said, balling the paper from my second taco. RV was looking at the bag of tacos.

"I'm not drunk," RV said. "Are there any tacos left? I don't see why you have to ground me when I'm not drunk."

"Two weeks is not a long time," Jewel said.

"Maybe not for you," RV said. She curled Frank's lip, exposing his teeth, trying to make him look enraged and vicious. She growled for him as she bared his teeth.

Saturday we cleaned up the yard, picked up twigs and raked acorns that had already started flying out of the trees. Frank was out with us, trotting around the perimeter of the yard, barking at squirrels, birds, other dogs, once in a while running back to Jewel to get petted. A couple of times RV showed on the porch and looked out, but she never came outside. One time she opened the screen and said, "I'm bored. Can we go to the video store?"

"We'll go later," Jewel said, dumping an armload of twigs

into a gray plastic wheelbarrow she'd bought at the Wal-Mart.

"I'm bored," RV said. "I want to go now."

"Later," Jewel said, wiping her forehead with the back of her hand, tucking a hair that had fallen out of her bandanna back into place.

"Oh, great," RV said. She smacked the screen door shut and stomped back into the house.

I was raking acorns and twigs and leaves into small piles a few feet apart in the yard. Jewel brought over a plastic bag, held it open, and I broomed the piles into the bag.

"She's fine," I said.

"I don't know, maybe."

"I'll take her to get a movie if you want," I said.

When we finished the cleanup we sat on the back steps and watched Frank prance around the yard. "I think we should go back to the casino and win more money," Jewel said.

"If we go back we'll lose. We won already."

"What, do you think you only win once? I don't believe that."

"So go. I'll stay here with Mr. Hyde, take her to get a movie, and you can go win a fortune."

"I don't know. I'll think about it," Jewel said.

When we went inside, RV was stretched out on the couch, watching MTV. A nerdish, scraggly guy was screaming that his life was wretched, no one loved him, the world was empty, people were awful, nothing was fair. This with the usual hash of queer camera angles, nostril shots, loopy film scratches and the rest.

"It's a tough life," I said to RV.

"Shh," RV said. "I'm listening."

Jewel went to the Paradise about nine. I took RV to Blockbuster to see what was rentable. She got a movie called *Kids* which I didn't know anything about. I got a fifties French movie called *Bob le Flambeur* that had raves on the box. We started with her movie, but after a few minutes I popped the cassette out of the VCR. It was grotesque stuff — teens and preteens in New York fucking, getting fucked, getting drunk, fucking more, talking about fucking. That was it. I was certain it was one hundred percent accurate. RV didn't need to see it.

"What're you doing?" she said.

I scratched my head. "Uh, what's the rating on that? Oh, never mind, we're not watching it. We need to get Jewel on that. What is that about, anyway?"

"It's about us," RV said. "Mom'll let me see it. C'mon. I'll watch it in my room if you want me to."

"Let's try the other one."

"What is it?"

"It's French," I said.

"Oh great," she said. "Just what I need." She had Frank in a headlock down at her end of the couch.

I switched the movies and punched Play.

Bob le Flambeur was a heist movie about a small-time French hood and his cronies trying to knock over a casino. RV lasted until the English credits came up.

"Oh, no kidding," she said, tossing Frank on his back on the couch. "*Bob the Gambler*? This is about gambling? That's so not interesting." She headed for her room.

I watched a few minutes, then decided to wait for Jewel, so I cut the VCR and flipped through the cable channels, stopping to watch bits of this and that — a standoff with some white supremacists, some NFL football trades, a bit of Jewel's favorite cooking show with a guy who looked as if his name ought to be Garson Linguine, a couple of R-rated nudie shows on Showtime and Cinemax, something on *Wings*, pops of C-SPAN and religious programming. At midnight I stretched out with the idea of watching a Bette Davis movie that had just started. Frank was at the other end of the couch, already asleep.

Bette Davis didn't last. I was switching again. I watched a soft-core thing on Showtime about a woman cop who turned vigilante and had a super car that turned itself from a red Corvette into a black Porsche when she was on a mission. Then I got some religious stuff, a bearded monk, Geraldo doing *O.J.: A Look Back* — I was thinking maybe there ought to be some licensing fees involved. Then there was some other talk show where some woman was angry that people didn't do their jobs the way they had in the fifties. The host wanted to know how this woman knew that, and the woman said she just knew, she'd seen movies about it. Then I caught some of *The Site* on MSNBC, which was sort of frightening because it seemed like the future, eighteen-year-olds taking themselves seriously, explaining things to the rest of us, hopelessly unaware of themselves. Some of the stuff was interesting, though, and that was scarier.

"Hey, Bob the Gambler," RV said, coming out of her room. "Mom's still at the casino? When's she getting home?"

I caught the lights of the car swinging across the living room wall as Jewel pulled into the driveway. I rolled off the couch and said, "I believe that would be now." I holstered the TV remote and went to the back door to meet Jewel. RV came with me.

Jewel was slow getting out of the car. She was sitting in it with the car door propped open and one foot out on the ground. She was counting money. RV opened the screen and went out.

"What's all this?" she said.

"What I got left," Jewel said. "How're you, baby?" She hugged RV.

"Will you make me some macaroni?" RV said.

"Sure, baby. Give me a minute here."

RV spun away and went back into the house. "I'll be in my room," she said. "O.K.? Say hello to Bob."

"Got it," Jewel said, shaking her head. "This was stupid. I got killed. Wait'll you see my ATM receipts, my credit-card receipts, the checks I wrote. Who's Bob?"

"Me," I said. "Her new name for me. You wrote checks? How much have you got there?"

"Eight hundred," she said. "But I bought in for twice that. I have to add it up."

"So you lost eight?"

"I was going for the fences. Played five-dollar slots. Played tens a couple times, two hundred worth. This guy next to me hit on a ten, not the one I played, and got three grand. So I thought maybe I could do that." She closed and locked the car, headed inside with a wad of money and her purse in one hand and a paperback in the other.

"What's the book?" I said, holding the door.

She flapped it into my chest. "Blackjack book. They say blackjack's your best odds against the casino. I'm thinking about our future."

"You want me to get you something?"

"How about some macaroni?" she said. "Just kidding. I'll fix RV, then figure the loss, then go to sleep. I was ahead once, seven hundred, so I thought I would live forever."

"Have you heard of this movie *Kids*?" I said.

"Oh, Jesus," she said. "You got that?"

"We didn't watch it. I cut it off. It's grisly."

I opened the refrigerator and looked for something to snack on while Jewel fixed macaroni for RV. Then she sat down on a stool in the kitchen and flattened out her various receipts, toting up how much she had invested in the night's gambling. It turned out that she'd bought two thousand and fifty dollars, so she was down twelve-fifty for the night.

"So what?" I said. "You won that last time. You're even."

"I know. But I was ahead. It was sort of fun — there was this guy who kept winning. He must have won six or seven thousand. That was great, I just wish it was me."

"Tell me tomorrow, huh? I'm dead. I almost fell asleep on the couch."

"Me too," she said.

"But I want to hear," I said. I put my arm around her and kissed her cheek, then kissed her lips. They were soft. Softer than usual.

I went to see my mother that weekend. Her house was in Bay St. Louis, thirty minutes west along the coast highway. To get there, I had to pass the spot where Jayne Mansfield was killed in a three A.M. car crash. Mother was leaning against the chain-link fence by the driveway, fingering the decorative scroll bolted onto the top of the gate. She was looking across Torch Street at the neighbor's garage, where a group of eight or nine people were having a Sunday afternoon barbecue. She waved me out of her line of sight as I came up the drive. I looked over my shoulder to see what she was studying.

"The Terlinks," she whispered when I got to the gate. "Johnson Terlink and his wife, Emma, their two children, Rita and Herman. I've never said a word to them. Somebody's with them over there. See that fancy rent car?"

"Somebody like who?" I said, going into the yard and locking the gate behind me.

Mother kicked at Bosco, the tiny dog who kept winding around her legs, in and out, panting, occasionally making tiny barking noises.

She'd moved to Bay St. Louis two years before because she

wanted a change in her life. My father didn't want any change, so there was some haggling, and she ended up moving with the idea of trying it out in Mississippi, maybe getting it set up for him to come, too. She wanted to get out of the house more, so she worked three nights a week at a tiny local hospital, St. Mary's, rolling patients over, wedging pillows under them, cleaning bedpans, changing drips and catheter bags. She'd trained as a nurse, though now she was just a glorified volunteer. My father wasn't all that healthy, and when she left he had to hire a nursing service. But with all of that they weren't divorced, just living apart, and I figured sooner or later he'd move in order to be with her. Otherwise, she'd go back. Still, it was messy watching my parents get suddenly headstrong in their golden years. I tried to dodge as much of it as I could.

The neighborhood was down-at-the-heels wood-frame buildings — lapped siding, painted white or gray or light yellow, with contrasty trim — one of the least-gentrified parts of the coast. Lots of weeds. The yards were thick with weeds, tricycles, colorful volleyballs, soccer balls, plastic doodads, dogs, worn-down-to-the-dirt dog runs. A kite twirled on the telephone wire behind the Terlinks' house. The kite had been there since my mother moved in.

The house on Torch Street was six blocks from the water, and if I went out into the street and leaned over and looked hard, I could see a thumbnail of Gulf under the heavy arch of trees.

"I should have introduced myself before this," she said, watching the kite flap like an unhinged bird caught in the wires.

She had six hours to spend with me before work. "How come you're not at the casino?" she said. "Figured you'd be over there going for it all."

"You've been talking to Jewel?" I asked.

"I've been talking," she said.

The tall guy on the Terlinks' driveway laughed loud. He looked familiar. "You want to order pizza?" I asked. "How about from Don't Nobody Eat Pizza?"

"Stand right here and look at this, will you?" she said. "I think we got John Larroquette here."

"Oh yeah? What's he doing?" I said.

"I don't know. I'm not sure it's him, but there's a guy looks like him, tall, that brush-hair thing, spiky, comes in this million-dollar rent car. I'm not sure, though."

"So walk on across," I said.

"That's your answer to everything. Walk right up," she said. "I don't want to meet him, I only want to know if it's him. So take a look-see and tell me if you can ID him. I don't ask too damn much."

"And you deserve the world," I said, kissing her forehead.

I leaned on the fence, squinted hard a minute, then said, "I give up. Could be. Let's head in." I tried to steer her to the back door. "I need to talk."

She shucked my hand. "Go out in the drive like you're getting something from your car."

"What makes you think it's him? Why do you care, you a *Cheers* fan or something? Wasn't he on *Cheers*?"

"Oh, like you don't know," she said. "*Night Court*. But he's had his own show for a couple years. He reminds me of your father."

"Yeah, so does Batman." I was wearing jeans and a 6XL gray T-shirt I'd ordered from the King Size catalog, and I didn't want to meet anybody. I walked around a bush at the corner of the house. "You need to come gambling, Mother. That's what. The other day we saw somebody there."

"Somebody?"

"Somebody famous. I don't remember who it was. Country singer, maybe. Johnny Paycheck or something. He was sitting on a stool with his butt showing. We called him Johnny Butt Crack."

"How very elegant and surprising, Raymond," she said. She tapped the ground in front of her with her toe. "Come here a minute."

My hair popped up from a breeze that came and went. I sat on the back steps and looked at her yard, which was like a small field where you might find an abandoned refrigerator and a few of the victim's body parts.

Bosco bit a low limb on a dark green bush, wagged his head back and forth until he'd torn the limb off, then ran around with the thing in his mouth, daring her to chase. She feinted at the dog and he dodged away.

I held my T-shirt at the hem, staring down at myself.

"You're a big fella," she said. "What're you, thirty-eight? Weren't you successful in that architecture business for about a minute? Shouldn't you be at some club with some fancy cut-throat home builder or something? The comptroller of the currency. Where's Jewel, anyway? I thought she was coming."

"She's sleeping. We were gambling until six this morning."

"Just like your father," she said.

I got up and opened the screen door, then shut my eyes, rubbed my hand through my hair several times, holding my head. "I'm not," I said. "I've never been. I don't know why you say that, you know I'm not."

"Mighty touchy," she said. She sat on the ground, gathering her skirt.

"Don't sit in the dirt, Mother," I said.

"He called yesterday, you know."

"What'd he say?"

"Said he missed me. I said I missed him, too."

"Do you?"

"Sure do. I'd like to get him to move over here, but he's a stubborn somebody."

"Come inside," I said. "I'll fix you something to eat — a toasted cheese sandwich. Would you like that?"

"No, thank you. I want to know if that's John Larroquette."

"It's not," I said.

"I saw him on Leno. He's from Louisiana. He visits his cousin in Mississippi, his only cousin. They have barbecues. That's what he told Jay."

I went down the steps into the yard and reached out to help my mother up. Bosco dropped the twig and hopped at her lap.

"I could talk to Mrs. Terlink about her dogs," Mother said.

"What dogs?"

"She raises Chihuahuas. That's what Laura told me. Laura next door?" She thumbed to her left where Laura lived. "Says Mrs. Terlink raises Chihuahuas. Says she's got maybe twenty-five Chihuahuas over there."

"I haven't seen *one*," I said.

"You haven't looked."

"I've looked before and I never saw a single Chihuahua," I said. "Are you coming inside? Tell you what, you come in and I'll go out like I'm getting the mail, and if it's him, I'll come get you and we'll go meet him, get his autograph."

"It's Sunday."

"Maybe you forgot yesterday," I said.

"What if they saw me get it yesterday?"

"Then we're putting something out for tomorrow, for the guy to pick up."

She smiled at me as she got to her feet. She was in her sixties, tall, thin, wearing a pale-blue-striped shirtwaist. She'd worn dresses like that all her life. "You know, I like you pretty well. You're a pleasure." She gave me a hug.

"Thank you," I said.

She finger-combed my hair over my head, left to right, until it felt like derelict hair. "You need to get some air to your skull here. These roots are weeping."

Inside, she sat on an old green stool by the stove. I made her an open-face sandwich of Rainbow bread and wrapper cheese. She took some cheese to feed Bosco, made him stand up on his hind legs and go around in circles, then dropped cheese strips from shoulder height to see if he could catch them. Most of the time the cheese went right past him, smacking the floor.

She walked out to the living room and stood at the front window, pulling back the curtain, peering across the street. "I think that's him," she said. "I'm almost certain that's him."

"Jesus, will you forget it?" I said. "Come eat your sandwich."

"Is it ready?" she said.

"No," I said.

"Let's go out in the car. We can get really close then, on the way out and the way back."

"I thought you wanted a sandwich. I'm making a sandwich for you. Are you going to eat?"

In the living room, she picked up three copies of *Family Circle* magazine and gathered some of Bosco's toys — a pink ball with a pebbled surface, a plastic bone the size of her forearm, and a book he liked to chew. She tossed all three toys into a basket in the corner of the living room where Bosco's things were kept.

Bosco wouldn't go near the basket. When he wanted a toy he'd walk up and stand a foot away, whimpering, looking back over his shoulder at Mother. It would have been easy for him to step up, put a paw on the basket, tip it over. But he never did that. He whimpered. Sometimes a toy went under a chair or the bench she had in the entry hall, and Bosco would do the same thing — stand and whimper. He was afraid the furniture was going to jump him. I liked that about him.

"Ready," I called. She came in the kitchen and ate her cheese sandwich. I had a peanut butter sandwich and stood at the window by the sink looking out at Laura's house.

"Snakes over there," Mother said.

"Huh?" I said.

"Laura came last week, told me the yard guy found a snake in the back, chased it under a tree stump. She had Animal Control come out, but they wouldn't touch it because it was under the stump. They said if it was out in the open they'd handle it, but underground was a whole different story, said it was her responsibility. Out in the open, they'd take it. Otherwise, no dice."

"That's a big help," I said.

"She was warning me about Bosco, to keep him out of the yard," she said. "Said it was a copperhead. I went and looked, stuck a broom handle in all the holes in that stump, but I didn't find it. She wanted to put gas on the stump and burn it. She's mad at me ever since the police came."

Two months before, the police had come to the house to talk about a case they were working on. Some pizza delivery guy was raping women. They called the guy the Pizza Rapist. They wanted to know how often she ordered pizza and from which pizza places. Two plainclothes policemen in cheap brown suits. They came in and sat in the living room with her, and in the middle of things, Laura had arrived.

Mother had called to tell me the story.

Laura wanted to come in but Mother wouldn't let her because the cops were there to talk to her, not Laura. If they'd wanted to talk to Laura, they'd have gone next door.

Laura was sixty-two, part-time assistant manager at the K & B drugstore in the old mall. She was thinking about going back to college.

"I'm watering the beds out front," Mother announced, opening the front door. She'd finished her sandwich and collected a straw hat and sunglasses. She looked back at me and I shook my head.

"Leave it, will you?"

"Let me water," she said.

"You can water if you want to. But don't stare over there the whole time."

"I won't. I'll be careful. Besides, I've got these glasses. They can't tell where I'm staring."

"That'll be great," I said. "They're not going to have any idea. You got them fooled. They will think you are out there watering and nothing more, Mother."

"Well, drive me somewhere, then."

"Fine," I said. "Where?"

"I don't care as long as we go in the car, so we can go by the driveway over there and see if it's him."

"What if it is?" I said.

"I've decided if it's him I want to meet him," she said. "I'd like to take him dancing."

"Forget it." I fell on the green couch. "He doesn't dance."

"Does. On Leno. And he has a wife. She's very English."

"Oh yeah?" I said.

"That's what he said. He said his wife was very English."

"She's probably too English."

"She was upset because he was having this barbecue with his cousin. He was in the garage like these people. It was cooler in the garage, he said, that's why they were in there. Then the English wife comes up and whispers that he's a redneck. That's what he said on Leno. He seemed like a really nice guy."

"I'm sure he's a peach," I said.

"We might go to the drugstore."

"We're not going to the drugstore unless you really need to."

"Garbage bags. Food for Bosco. Coffee."

So we toddled out to her car, an Oldsmobile, green, from the eighties. She liked to drive when we went anywhere, but I insisted.

"Well, go slow," she said as I backed out.

"I'm going as slow as I can. If I go any slower, I'll be going too slow."

"You're going backwards. How can you go too slow?"

"Mother," I said. I crawled us past the Terlinks' house, past the driveway, and she stared up the drive and waved at the Terlinks. They all waved back from the deep shadow of the garage.

"Go back," she said. "I couldn't see."

"I can't go back now."

"Stop. I'll go look in the trunk for something."

"No, Mother. That's it. We'll check them on the way back."

Half a dozen houses down the street there was a brown horse standing in somebody's front yard, tied to a tree. The horse had a bridle on, but that was all — no saddle. Nobody was paying attention to this horse standing there by the tree. It was caked with pale mud.

"What's with this?" she said, pointing out her window.

"Horse," I said. "Somebody's got a horse."

"Well, they should wash it," she said. "Look at that. It's hot, its feet are clogged with mud, its mane. They ought to get somebody over here to wash it."

"Should we go to the mall?" I said.

"Yes," she said.

The old strip mall was out on Whorton Road, off Highway 90. Two police cars were nosed into the drainage ditch with their blue lights flashing. An ambulance was tilted off the side of the road.

"What's this?" she said.

When we got close enough, we saw that somebody had driven a panel van into the ditch. Somebody else had gone in right after and landed on top of the van. That person was still sitting in his car, slumped over to the side. The driver of the panel van was strapped on a board alongside the van, deep in the ditch, surrounded by cops and paramedics.

"It doesn't look good," she said. "I've seen that head get-up on *ER*. See the way they've got the Styrofoam thing around his head there?"

"You want some yogurt?" I said. "I'm stopping at the yogurt place."

"Fine," she said. "Look at this guy in the Cadillac. He's perched up there. Why don't they get him out? He looks bad."

"You'd be bad if you were parked on top of a van in your Cadillac."

"What if those cars explode?" she said.

I drove into the strip center and angled toward the yogurt shop. At the drive-in window I asked her what she wanted. She said fat-free chocolate in a waffle cone. I got a vanilla cup and an oatmeal cookie. When the yogurt came, I paid, then drove out to the edge of the parking lot and stopped, rolling the windows down. From where we were sitting, we could see the wreck off to our left, the police and the ambulance, the road in front of us, and two shopping centers across the street. I left the car running, and I left the air conditioning going even though the windows were down.

"I don't remind you of my father, do I?" I said after a few minutes.

"Some ways. What's wrong, you don't like him?"

"I like him fine, but he didn't do so well, you know? Like in the larger scheme of things. With you, with the rest of the world. He had his problems."

"He did all right," she said. "Ran out of steam, is all. You could do worse."

"You think so?"

"Sure. He's a champ compared to most men. He's not stupid and he never hit me. You people these days whine so much."

"Heard that," I said, dipping my spoon into the yogurt. "You know, I'm doing the laundry when we get back. Dishes, too. I'm doing dishes and laundry."

"Fine. Do 'em all night long," she said.

"I like water. The way water sounds running. I could do dishes for hours — water's warm and soapy, you know, you've got a good sponge and you get some soap in that and rub it on the plates and the plates get slippery and everything gets slippery so there's some danger."

"You're sounding like him," she said. "Maybe you're too weird."

"Sometimes when Jewel's gone I wash dishes and clothes at the same time, so I have the washer running — sometimes the washer and the dryer — and I'm doing dishes, too. That's great. I really like that. That does it for me."

"Now that *really* reminds me of him," she said. She looked out her window at a yellow dog that had its nose stuffed in a Burger King sack. The dog lifted the sack up, throwing its head back so that it could get deeper into the bag. It was walking around on the striped concrete with this bag on its face.

"I hope that guy in the van doesn't die," I said.

"Me too," she said. "So what do you want for dinner? Are you staying for dinner?"

"We just had sandwiches and yogurt. I can't think yet."

"You could barbecue. We could do that in the driveway, like the Terlinks. Maybe they could come over."

"Yeah. Two years and suddenly you're inviting them for barbecue."

We were quiet in the car finishing the yogurt. The main thing I heard was the smacking of our lips. When I finished, I squashed the cookie bag into the cup, broke the plastic spoon and put it in the cup, too, then opened my door and set the cup on the concrete.

"Why do you want to do that?" she said. "Here. Give it to me."

"I'm leaving it here," I said. "It's a gift. I don't have any dirty diapers or chicken bones to leave, so this is the best I can do."

"Oh, Jesus. Raymond, open the door and pick that up."

"I'm not." I backed the car in a half-circle.

She reached over and struggled with the steering wheel, trying to force me to drive back and pick up the cup, but I turned the wheel in the other direction and drove diagonally across the lot.

"I need to get a magazine," I said.

"I need to get home," she said. "We need to solve this problem once and for all."

"Dinner?" I said.

"No," she said. "Not dinner. I've got chicken at home. I stewed some chicken. You can have that if you want something. I'm having a salad. Or we can barbecue."

I drove more cautiously than I needed to.

She said, "You kind of drive like him. There isn't that much difference. If I shut my eyes, if I couldn't see who was in the driver's seat, I could imagine being with Hopper."

That was my father's name, Hopper. "Thanks, Mother," I said, speeding up.

The Oldsmobile had been my father's car. He gave her the car and bought the house in Bay St. Louis. I wished he had moved with her so that I could watch them together in their dotage, shrinking like a matched pair. I figured Mother would like a fancier house, but she didn't worry much about the one on Torch Street. She kept it clean, and it had that nice old-house smell about it. In the summers, when the ceiling fans were going and the attic fan was on and a breeze was being pulled through the open windows, I could close my eyes and imagine being at my grandparents' house in Galveston when I was a kid, remember the way things smelled, the way the air moved. It had a certain sweet mustiness I remembered. That was how Mother's house smelled on its best days.

There wasn't anything left of the Terlinks' barbecue when we got home. The rent car was gone, the garage doors were shut. There were a few dim lights inside, squinting out through tight-cranked mini-blinds.

Mother rolled her barbecue grill out of the garage onto the driveway, took off the lid, removed the cooking rack, went back into the garage for charcoal briquettes and poured them into the bottom, sprayed them with Gulf lighter fluid, then walked around looking at her flower beds while she waited for the lighter fluid to seep into the briquettes.

I went inside and came out to tell her there were steaks in the freezer. "I think I'll defrost them in the microwave," I said.

"Are there vegetables?" she said. "I want spinach."

When I came back out, she had opened an aluminum folding chair on the driveway and was sitting with a hose, spraying water onto the flower bed between her property and Laura's. She had a five-dollar nozzle on the end of the hose. I held up two packs of frozen vegetables. "Corn or lima beans?"

"Both," she said. She released the trigger, closing the nozzle, and handed me the hose while she lit the charcoal. Then she put the cooking rack on top and scrubbed it with a wire brush, risking her skin in the flames. She sat down and took the hose back and started spraying again. There was a breeze that shifted the water from the spray slightly out of its path, and sometimes a mist flew back on us. It felt nice and cool. It felt refreshing. She swung the nozzle and sprayed the Oldsmobile and then started on the bed on the house side of the driveway. She kept an eye on the Terlinks' garage.

I went inside and put the vegetables on, wondering what made her want it to be John Larroquette. You could spend your whole life wanting something and never even come close.

A couple years before, when she was moving, she'd told me a secret about her life. When she married Hopper she was in love with a man she had met in nursing school. He was beautiful and powerful and smart. He knew that she loved him or at least that she had a crush on him. Sometimes he took advantage of it — touching her in ways that he shouldn't have, feeling her waist, holding her, even kissing her, or casually brushing against her at the school. It happened too often to be accidental, but that was as far as it went. Later he became the weatherman for the only TV station in Galveston.

On their wedding night, after she and my father had consummated their marriage, she watched this man she loved do the weather forecast on the TV. "He was so handsome," she said. "Television was in its infancy."

I came out with the steaks on a cookie sheet. I'd put a lot of Worcestershire sauce on them. "How long?" I said, holding the cookie sheet up on five fingers as if I were a waiter.

"Any minute," she said. "Coals are gray."

"I did the vegetables in the microwave. You want to eat by the TV?"

"Sure," she said. "What's on?"

"I don't know," I said. "It could be anything. It's Sunday — there's probably some kind of special."

"I never watched his show anyway," she said.

"What?"

"Larroquette," my mother said. "He seemed like a nice guy when I saw him on TV. I liked him. He talked like somebody you could like. He pinched his fingers together and said he was a redneck about that far under the skin. It didn't seem to bother him. He laughed when he said it. That's such a wonderful thing for a famous man to do."

I stood looking at her for a few seconds, then brought the cookie sheet down and handed it to her. I pulled a cooking fork out of my back pocket and handed that to her as well. I took the hose out of her hand and spritzed it up in the air so that it rained lightly, as if the sky were hesitant to disturb us.

RV was grounded again, this time for a week, on account of her grades, but the grounding wasn't the rough-and-tumble stuff that it had once been. She started riding us about a dance party at Mallory's church, scheduled for Wednesday night. She whined all Tuesday and all afternoon Wednesday until Jewel finally gave in, on condition Mallory's parents were driving and were going to be at the dance. I called Mrs. Miles late Wednesday afternoon to check on the plan.

"Oh, yes, of course, absolutely," Mrs. Miles said. "It's my party. I'll be looking after the girls. You don't need to worry at all. I love these girls. I take care of them as if they are my own, even the ones who aren't."

"We just wondered whether you were going to be there," I said.

"Absolutely. I'm there for the girls, always. And your daughter is so cute. Now, how old is she? Is she fourteen? Is she thirteen?"

"Fourteen," I said.

"She's so cute. When she spends the night I love it."

I tried to remember the last time RV stayed at Mallory's.

It had been a while. RV and Mallory weren't such great friends these days, and I was glad because Mallory was an unpleasant girl who I figured was a bad influence. She was a liar, a schemer, an ugly brat, and the less RV saw of her the better. Of course, RV and Mallory were on-again off-again, so there really was no hope. No sooner would they split up than they'd make up.

Sometimes Jewel and I tried to figure what we could do to permanently ice the friendship. We were totally unprofessional about it.

"Thanks very much, Mrs. Miles," I said. "You're driving? You want me to bring RV over?"

"I'll fetch her," Mrs. Miles said. "I like to do that when I drive the girls."

"O.K.," I said. "She'll be ready."

"They'll have a wonderful time," she said. "They're so cute, the girls, when they go to these dances and stand in their little groups, chattering and looking at the boys. Waiting for the boys to make some overture."

"Uh-huh," I said.

"When I was fourteen it was just the same," Mrs. Miles said, sighing audibly. She sounded as if she might be having a slight bronchial problem. "Oh, well. Gone forever. I'll have little uh, RV, back to you by ten-thirty."

"Thanks very much."

"Oh, it's a pleasure. I live vicariously through those girls — do you ever do that?"

I paused long enough to realize I wasn't supposed to actually answer the question. "Yes, of course. It's one of the great pleasures of parenthood, isn't it?"

"Oh, I think so," Mrs. Miles said. "Absolutely."

RV was ready at five-fifteen. When Mrs. Miles arrived an hour later, RV opened the door and walked out, leaving me in the doorway. I waved at Mrs. Miles and the five girls who were already in the car. They were giggling and jumping around as if playing games in the back seat. Only one girl was in the front. She waved as RV walked down the brick walk. I stood in the door and smiled as they drove away. Nobody in the car looked back.

The blackjack book told you how to play every combination of cards you could get versus whatever card the dealer had. Jewel and I practiced a couple of nights, and we got the idea, though we didn't have the plays memorized. The book said don't play until you know basic strategy like your wife's name. But it came with a credit-card-size cheat sheet that you could take to the casino, so the author knew we weren't going to memorize everything before hitting the tables.

After RV went to the dance, Jewel dealt herself a few hands of blackjack — playing the player and the dealer as well. She played three hands against one dealer's hand and shuffled when she got to the end of the deck. After a time she decided to run over to the casino.

I went with her, just to observe.

She cashed a check for three hundred, then looked for a table. Everybody was having a lot of fun. There was laughter. Up and down the rows of table games there were raucous outbursts as somebody won something and gave somebody else a high-five. High-fives went all around a table. She took a seat at a table where only one guy, a farmer type, was playing.

"I've never played," she announced to the dealer, who was a young man about twenty whose name tag said "Rocky."

"Never?" he said.

The farmer guy looked up and squinted. I looked to see if he had any oats on him, then took the empty seat next to Jewel.

"Played at home, that sort of thing," she said, handing him a hundred-dollar bill. He gave her two green chips and ten reds.

"I'll walk you through it," Rocky said. "For a few hands, anyway."

"Walk me forever. I'm going to need all the help I can get."

"Put your bet here," he said, tapping the circle on the felt in front of her. "Minimum five dollars, one red."

She put a chip into the circle. The farmer was playing three circles, a green chip in each. He was on the other side of the table, playing the first three spots. She was in the last seat on the left side of the table, me on her right. Rocky dealt cards, two face-up to each hand, face-up and face-down to himself. She got nineteen. Rocky had a six showing. The farmer had a blackjack, a pair of fours, and a king-two.

The dealer paid the blackjack right away. "Thirty-seven dollars fifty cents for a quarter," he said, turning to Jewel. "Blackjack pays time and a half."

"Got it," Jewel said.

The farmer put a second green chip by his fours. Rocky pulled the cards apart and started dealing to the first one. He dealt a seven and the farmer put out a third green chip, and Rocky said, "Doubling on eleven."

"Monkey," said the farmer, tapping his four-seven. Rocky dealt him a king. Then the guy tapped the next card. He got a five, put another quarter chip out, and got a nine. He waved back and forth over the king-deuce.

Rocky turned to her. "You don't want a card. See, you assume I've got a ten down, so with a six, I've got to hit. Thirty-two cards per deck bust me."

"Right," Jewel said.

"You gotta give me a hand signal," Rocky said. "Go back and forth above your cards. For the cameras." He flicked his head toward the ceiling.

Jewel waved for him. Rocky turned over his card. It was a jack. He dealt himself another jack.

"Winner, winner," said the farmer. It sounded like "wiener, wiener." He popped himself in the forehead with his palm.

"You win," Rocky said, putting a five-dollar chip beside the one she had in the circle, then paying the farmer's bets.

"Couldn't be easier," Jewel said. "I have a great future in the game." She left a red chip in the circle and pulled one back. Rocky collected the cards, slid them into the plastic discard rack, and started dealing again.

I watched her play for two hours, betting reds. Once in a while I played, but mostly I watched. She got ahead seventy-five dollars. She had a twenty-five-dollar bet out when we heard her paged on the casino loudspeaker.

She started to pick up her chips.

Rocky said, "Don't worry. I'll watch them."

She looked at him for a second, then at the farmer. "Where's a phone?"

Rocky pointed to a mirrored column two tables down that had a cream-colored phone mounted on its side. "That'll do," he said.

"I'll go," I said. "You go on playing."

I went to the phone and called the operator and then was clicked through. It was RV, calling from the dance. "How'd you know we were here?"

" 'Cause you're Bob the Gambler," she said. "You winning?"

"A little. Are you all right?"

"Sure. Is my mom there?"

I told her to hang on, then let the phone dangle down to the floor on its curly white cord while I went to get Jewel. "It's RV," I said to her. "She wants to talk to you."

"Play my cards, O.K.?" She handed me the cards. Rocky got nervous about keeping the cards on the table and playing with one hand.

"Gotcha," I said. We had thirteen and he had a ten. I asked for a card, scratching our thirteen on the felt like a pro.

When Jewel came back to the table she said, "One of us has to go home. They're coming in early."

"I can get a cab," I said. "I'm tired anyway."

"Great," Jewel said. "You're sure you don't mind? I'm kind of getting the hang of this."

"You're a regular Pegleg Pete," I said. "Are we still grounding her again after tonight? I don't see why."

"Why are they having a dance in the middle of the week, anyway?" she said.

"You said it was a church thing, right? That's why Mallory's dedicated and loving mother was involved."

"Right," Jewel said. "I forgot."

"She loves the girls. She really, really loves the girls. Really. What time are they getting home?"

"Ten. What time is it now?" Jewel said.

"Nine-thirty," I said.

"You roll," Jewel said.

I stood in the kitchen. The house was empty. I looked out the door of the kitchen into the living room and dining room, and what I wanted was to take off my shoes and sit on the sofa and watch television, but I was worried about Mrs. Miles. Then I decided I didn't care about Mrs. Miles. She could come in and sit in my lap if she wanted to. I got a beer, went to the living room, wedged off my shoes, found the remote, and sat down. Then Frank scratched on the back door. I went to let him in, wiped his paws with a towel. He'd worn the perimeter of the yard down to the original dirt, so we kept a towel for his feet. I locked the door. Frank and I went to the living room and got on the couch. I flipped channels. At a couple of spots I clicked the sound on, but mostly I went silently. I'd been through twice, my feet on the coffee table, when Frank got up and put his head in my lap. I stared at the wall above the television and petted the dog. I remembered the fight Jewel and I had over the sofa. I said it was uninteresting and ugly. She said it was comfortable. I said that we shouldn't buy it, it was uninteresting and ugly. She said she wanted it. I was glad I lost.

RV hit the door at nine-fifty, Mrs. Miles in tow. "Hi," she said when I opened the door. "I'm Verona Miles, Mallory's mother. You must be Ray?"

"I must be," I said to her.

She laughed at that. "Well, your little RV is *such* a darling," she said. "She's so perfectly behaved. So quiet."

"She's quiet?" I said, stepping aside so RV could get into the house. Mrs. Miles wasn't letting go of me. I thought of yanking my hand out of hers.

"Did you have a good time at the dance?" I said, looking after RV, who was already in her room.

"They had such a wonderful time," Mrs. Miles said. "They did all the little things they do, and then we left early, and I took them to Baskin-Robbins."

"That was very sweet," I said, leaning back.

"I hope we're not late," she said.

"Not at all." I looked at my watch. "You're right on time. Early, even."

"Well, they wanted to go," she said. "I always like to be there so if they want to go, they can go." She gave me a broad smile and one final ripple on the hand, then released me and took a step back.

"Thanks very much for taking her," I said. "I'm sure Jewel will be calling for a report."

"That would be splendid," Mrs. Miles said. "I can tell her everything. We haven't talked for a long while."

"Uh-huh." I was waving at her, although she was only four feet away.

"Well, see you later. Bye-bye," she said. She turned and walked down the steps, out toward her car.

I locked up, then knocked on RV's bedroom door. "You O.K. in there?"

"I'm fine," she said. "I'm changing."

"Did you have a good time?" I said.

"No. It was stupid. All these stupid kids. I wish I hadn't gone," she said.

"That's too bad," I said.

"Where's Mom?" RV said.

"I think she's at the store or something," I said. "She'll be home shortly."

"She's still at the casino?" RV said.

I looked at the paint on the door to RV's room. "So what if she is?" I said it to the door.

"Nothing," RV said. "Never mind."

"Are you coming out?"

"In a minute," RV said.

I went to the kitchen looking for a piece of Edward's key lime pie, a new obsession. I couldn't get enough. There was always something I couldn't get enough of, in the food line of things. For weeks it had been Edward's key lime. It didn't taste like key lime pie, but that didn't matter. The pieces came in individual wedge-shaped boxes. When I started buying the pie that way I couldn't figure out how to open the boxes, so I ended up ripping them apart. Then Jewel showed me how to press on both sides of the box and open the top like the hood of a car. Amazing. There were no markings, no instructions. I was thrilled that she had figured it out.

I put pie on a plate and returned to the couch. Frank was interested in the pie.

"Save you a bite," I said, pointing my fork at the dog. He stuck his muzzle right up next to the plate, ran his tongue around the front of his mouth but didn't touch anything. "Careful," I said, giving him the stare.

RV came out of her room in boxer shorts and a T-shirt. "Is there dinner?"

"Not that I know of," I said. "There might be something out there."

"I could have macaroni," she said. She didn't stop on her way through the living room. Frank got off the sofa and started to follow her into the kitchen, then turned and looked at me.

"More pie," I said, struggling to my feet.

Jewel bought blackjack books, lots of them, we had a dozen, then eighteen, then some she sent away for. She said it was the only library she'd ever wanted. She sat in bed every night in her own T-shirt and boxers and read about blackjack. We seemed to have all the important books on the game in bed with us every night. I was usually a book behind her. The casino had become a steady routine for us. We went often, a couple of times a week or more, and we stayed longer and longer. We were betting a lot bigger, we had gotten up to the twenty-five-dollar tables, and sometimes bet up to a hundred dollars a hand. Occasionally she went alone, or I went alone. I tried craps for a while, played Come and Don't Come, placed some sixes and eights, even laid some of the proposition bets the books said to stay away from. No luck anywhere.

One night early in October, after dropping six hundred at craps, I sat down at a cheap blackjack table, playing five-dollar chips. In a couple of hours I won back more than half of the six hundred. Jewel was off playing ten-dollar slots. When we left we were only three hundred down, two that I lost and one she dumped on dollar machines on the way out the door. In the car on the way home, she said, "This isn't working so well, is it?"

"We're not killing them," I said.

"You know, I mean, are you going to get some work?" she said. "I don't want to be pissy, but shouldn't you get some work, or close the office and work for somebody else?"

"What about playing blackjack for a living?"

"I'm a dead bitch," she said. "Why didn't I think of that? Hey, let's take a drive, ride the coast like we used to. What do you say?"

"You want to just drive?"

"Yeah. Head for Bay St. Louis, we'll go all the way. We'll go see your mother. It's a nice night, isn't it? There's fall or something in the air."

"I noticed that," I said. "Has this bite to it."

"Roll down the windows," she said, pointing toward the console where the electric-window buttons were.

I did the windows and settled in the driver's seat, enjoying the air whipping through my window. "I'm going to do something," I said. "Raymond Kaiser Design is kind of like being a pro bongo player."

"Is not. You do gorgeous work," she said. "We're just a little burned out, both of us, really. Things aren't as much fun as they used to be, you know? When we first got here."

"Fun doesn't know our name," I said. "You're still making money, though."

"That's not it. Everything's dull. Nature's dull, Frank is dull, daily life is dull. We're going through the motions. The casino's fun, but that's it."

The road in front wound around the coast and the wind swept sand across it, scalloping the highway and peppering my arm. Jewel held her hair back with one hand.

"I thought everything was O.K."

"Well, sure, it is," she said. "It's O.K., in this dull way. Plus, gambling isn't dull. That's all I'm saying."

"With the gambling you want to jack up the stakes, know what I mean?"

"You do?"

"Well, sure," I said. "I want to. The urge to push it all out there and let the cards do it is strong."

"Yeah, I've had that. And I'm going over there all the time, and when I'm not there, I'm thinking about it. At work I remember what it's like to hit two double bars and a double diamond on a five-dollar machine. Right in the middle of the day."

"The jones," I said, pulling into a gas station. "I want a beer. You?"

"Sure," Jewel said.

We parked under a huge wedge-shaped metal overhang and went into the store. I got a couple of beers from the cooler and Jewel pawed through the chips until she found something she wanted. We put everything on the counter and paid the woman the six bucks she asked for.

"You want a bag for that?" the woman asked. She had a submarine tattooed on her upper arm, bubbles coming out of it.

"Please," I said.

"Been at the boats?" the woman said, lowering the beers by their necks into the sack, tossing the Pringles in on top.

"What, we got poker chips stuck to us or something?" Jewel said, inspecting her chest, running her hands through her hair.

"Ah, you can tell after a while," the woman said. "People get a look. I go, too. I ain't criticizing. I'm probably going after I get off here tonight."

"Yeah?" Jewel said. "What do you play?"

"Slots, mostly. I hit ten thousand dollars one night. Next day I'm at the orthodontist with my baby girl. She's going to have the best teeth in six counties when we're done. Straight and just as white as could be. Look like a bathtub in there. Not like me."

She gave us a short demo of her teeth, which were brown and crooked and not all present, not even half.

"That doesn't look bad at all," Jewel said, pointing vaguely toward her own mouth.

I grabbed the sack and stepped away from the counter so Jewel could cut in front of me to the door. "Thanks," I said. "Good luck tonight."

"I could use it," the woman said. "Her teeth ain't the only problem we got."

We drove some more, then pulled up in a sandy parking zone alongside Highway 90, got out and crossed the road, headed toward the beach. It was like walking on beanbag chairs down there, but we got close to the water and sat.

"Slots giveth and slots taketh away," I said.

"They're good when they come in, aren't they? Nothing like that sound. Nothing."

"Gotta hit it first," I said. "Have you been tracking your win-loss?"

"Sort of," she said. "I've lost more than I've won. A thousand more, maybe. But I bang that double diamond once and I'm back on top."

"Playing five dollars?"

"Yeah. Tonight the guy next to me hit three triple diamonds with one coin. Seventy-five hundred. Something like that. Three *double* diamonds is five thousand dollars with one coin. I hit that."

"Five thousand dollars?"

"Yeah, I told you, didn't I? About ten days ago? I dumped it back into a twenty-five-dollar machine. I was thinking I'd kill them. It was their money, anyway."

"When it's in your pocket, it's yours."

"Yeah, I read that part, too," she said. "I'll get it back. Don't worry."

It was ten-thirty and the beach was empty. Out in front of us was a big black nothing, a couple of mustard-yellow lights sleepy on the horizon. Behind us the highway and, across that, a line of old houses and older trees. There was a chill in the air. I cut my eyes toward Jewel, then back at the Gulf.

"I'm down more than a thousand," I said. "Not much."

"So we're like, what, two grand in six weeks?"

"Something like that. Plenty of videos."

"It's not addiction," she said. "We're messing around. We're bored or something. You bored?"

"I don't have any work, Jewel. I'm doing nothing. I don't know, maybe I'm bored, sure. I ought to feel better than I do. You bored?"

"I guess. Except I like this." She pointed a finger at a small casino east of where we were sitting. "I don't want to lose everything we've got, though. You know how those stories go. Lawyer ends up driving a milk truck."

"That wouldn't be so bad," I said. "Start all over. This dealer was telling me about a guy who lost two hundred thousand last year. He's into them two hundred, but he owns clothing stores in Florida, so it doesn't matter. Two hundred thousand. Be nice, wouldn't it?"

We finished the beers and got back to the car, rode on toward Bay St. Louis. I stared at the faintly glowing dials on the dash. The Explorer rumbled under us. We passed the Grand Casino and the Lady Luck, both of which lit up the sky, washed it with colored light. "Maybe we should try them sometime," Jewel said.

"Not for me," I said. "Besides, it's your money."

"Oh, give it up, will you, Ray?" She turned around in the seat to face me. "Listen, I've got a slot system. I always cash out, no matter what I hit. I use fresh bills all the time so the machine thinks I'm a new player. It sort of works."

"I don't think so," I said. "Can you say, coincidence?"

"Maybe," she said. She draped her arm out the window a minute, stirring up the air. "I love it when they hit. You know the sound when they hit? That dingy sound, it's like faster, and contained somehow? That's a great sound. Happens like a fraction of a second before you know what you've hit, before you figure it out."

"The machine's thinking it wants to surprise you," I said.

"Thanks, Raymond," she said, twisting back and forth on the seat in a kind of Ray Charles solo.

We drove awhile without talking, and then at the stoplight at Plattner Road, she said, "What about RV? What are we going to do about her?"

"Spare the rod, I guess."

"How very seventies," she said.

"Oh yeah? Is it? What's nineties? What are we supposed to do?"

"I don't know," Jewel said. "The drinking business sure went away, as far as I can tell. She hasn't been drunk since that second time. Maybe she's over it. Maybe it was a momentary thing."

"She seems straight to me," I said.

"You don't sound convinced."

"No, I just don't have any idea," I said. "I mean, I could make some dire predictions about the wretched things to come, but I'd be doing it to protect myself in case they did come. I really don't know. She seems like a nice enough kid."

"How about an arranged marriage?" Jewel said. "Like for next year."

"I wish she'd talk to me more. We have this deal, this standoff thing, but I thought we were close anyway. Now sometimes

I think she's really ignoring me. She goes in her room, makes snide remarks. We probably should have washed her mouth out with soap when she was younger."

"That what Leona and Hop did?"

"Yep," I said. "Couldn't get the taste out of my mouth. You've got to admire those oldsters. They got shit done. Wasn't pretty, but they got it done."

"What else did they do?"

"I don't remember. I was spanked with a shingle, grounded, de-privileged, spanked more, sent to my room. Bludgeoned. Made to sleep with slugs."

Jewel flipped her head left and right to get the hair away. "So we're too easy on her now?"

"We're easier than they were."

"Yeah, and they were easier than their parents," Jewel said. "That's the way it probably goes."

"We're less disciplined. That's all I'm saying."

"That bitch is in chains when I get home," Jewel said.

We stopped at the Copa in Gulfport. It was a scabby white-washed cruise ship converted into a half-floating, half-tethered casino that vibrated like Dynamic Home Neck Massage. The floors were peaked some in the center. We played two-deck pitch blackjack, comparing cards, practicing. After an hour and a half, we had lost seven hundred.

"I'll hit the ATM," she said.

"That would help," I said. "We appear to be losing."

"Only a few hundred."

"Yeah, I forgot, we're made of money," I said. "Maybe I ought to call RV. What is it, eleven?"

"Quarter to twelve," she said, making a face.

"We need to be home? Get five more, and if that doesn't work, we'll go. I'll call her. Meet you back here?"

I found a phone and called. RV was watching MTV. I could hear it. "Hey, doll," I said. "You doing O.K.? You get something to eat?"

"Hey, it's Bob the G.," RV said. "Where you at? You shoot out to Vegas on an overnight jet?"

"We're at the Copa," I said. "In Gulfport. We took a drive and ended up here."

"You coming home any time?" RV said.

"Soon," I said. "Are you getting ready for bed? You've got school, don't you?"

"I'm doing homework, waiting for you guys."

"We're about to leave," I said.

"Hurry up. You're never here anymore."

"We're there. I guess we've been out some recently."

"Pretty soon I'll be the shells-and-cheese girl."

"Half an hour," I said. "O.K.?"

"Whatever."

When I got back to the table, Jewel was playing both our spots, twenty-five dollars each.

"She all right?" Jewel said.

"She's fine. She's waiting for us." I pulled the stack of greens over from in front of Jewel and put out two bets of a hundred dollars.

"What are you doing?"

"Trying to win our money back," I said. "Speeding things up."

Jewel brushed at the front of her T-shirt. "What, you missed the chapter where it says you can't win money back, you can't even think about winning money back, and if you do you've already lost?"

"Which book said that?" I said.

"Every one," she said.

The cards came. I hit one hand, stood on the other, lost both to a dealer who got twenty on four cards. I stacked and unstacked chips, measuring the stacks one against the other until they were equal. A hundred forty-five in each stack. I put the stacks on the spots, and the cards came again. Eighteen on one, nineteen on the other. I tucked the cards under the chips and put an arm around Jewel.

The dealer had a jack up. She picked it up and flipped her hole card with it. The hole card was another jack. I shoved away from the table.

"Sorry," the dealer said, already sweeping from right to left, collecting and racking the bets.

"That's it," I said.

"We have to go anyway." Jewel patted my back and started toward the entrance. "Let's roll."

"I need to try this once more," I said. "Maybe another five hundred and I can get it."

"C'mon. Forget that." She dragged me by the arm away from the table. "You said RV was waiting."

"You get the car. I'll meet you in a minute." I yanked my arm free and crossed toward the cashier.

Jewel followed me. "Ray. Come on now."

I turned abruptly. "Leave me the fuck alone, will you?"

She reeled as if hit, stared a minute, gave her head a shake.

"I'm doing this," I said. "I'll meet you in the car."

"That was pretty," she said, moving around me toward the entrance. "Fuck you, too."

"Jewel," I said. "C'mon. I'll be there in a flash."

She kept walking.

RV was asleep in her bed and the television was still blaring when we got home. I turned off the lights and television, arranged the sheets, kissed her forehead.

Jewel was in the bathroom. The tub was filling with pretty-sounding water. She brushed her teeth with the buzzing Sonicare. I walked in and asked if she wanted a beer. "Yes," she said, her mouth frothy with toothpaste.

I undid a couple of shirt buttons, flipped off my shoes, got two beers from the kitchen, and went to sit with her while she bathed. She was in the tub already. I put the seat down on the toilet, sat and stretched my legs.

"Sorry about that thing at the casino," I said. "I needed, I don't know, something. I mean, I was going to do it, and you —"

She flapped a washcloth at me. "Forget it," she said. "It was nothing. Fuck you, by the way."

"I got excited," I said. "Angry or something. I guess that's no excuse."

"No," Jewel said.

I stared at the mouth of my beer bottle thinking about ringworm, thinking about the kids I knew in grade school who had ringworm and had to wear stockings on their heads for weeks at a time. It had missed me, and I was still grateful, and fearful, thirty years later.

"Something came over me. I had to try it," I said. "The dog ate my homework."

"So you tried it," she said.

"I thought maybe I could turn it around."

"But, no. Instead you doubled our loss." She leaned back in the tub, resting her head against its edge, her knees up, twisted the washcloth into a tight knot, then opened it and placed it square on her chest, covering her nipples. She flipped water up onto the washcloth, using her hands as paddles. There was a scratch at the door.

"Frank," Jewel said.

I let him in and shut the door again. I scratched his ears and skull. When I sat down, he put his snout on the edge of the tub by Jewel's shoulder.

"You want some pets, bugs?" She shook water from her

hand and reached to stroke the dog's muzzle, clean his eyes, rub the top of his head. "Daddy was a big gambler tonight," she said. "He told me to get fucked. What do you think? Is that a way to talk? You want to get in this tub with me?"

Frank didn't answer. When she finished petting, he stayed in place a minute, then backed away and shook his head to throw off the water, then curled up with his back against the porcelain.

"I apologized," I said.

"I'm not used to you talking to me that way. It's shocking."

"I might have won," I said.

"That would have changed much," she said. "Let's go to bed and forget it. Call it a bad night."

"Was that." I dribbled the end of the beer into my mouth, then flipped the bottle end over end, catching it by its neck. I did that a couple of times before Jewel asked me to stop.

"It's not like this is a terrible loss. It's not like we can't afford it."

Jewel glanced at me. Her head was turned to the side, cocked off center. She was smiling, the faintest smile, and the water was beading on her chin, on her neck, on her shoulders, and what I thought was that she was great looking, like movie-perfect. Beautiful. What I thought was I was lucky. "I are dumb?" I said.

"Hey! Pinpoint thinking," Jewel said, drawing her hands out of the water and doing a strange finger gun.

"I'm a slow somebody."

"Tortoise," she said. "You're walking across the sand in the desert and there's a tortoise on its back, its feet scrambling in the air —"

"You forgive me?"

"Of course. I wouldn't be me if I didn't forgive you," she said.

"That's why it's worth it," I said. I leaned over the tub and kissed her. She wrapped a hand around my neck and held me there a long time. The beer bottles clinked against the side of the tub. The dog stretched and then leaned into the tub, sniffing our faces, licking at us in that way dogs have of not really getting you full on. We ignored him and took a minute to quit the kiss.

Then I said, "I'm going," and left them in the bathroom. I went to the kitchen, tossed my beer bottle, got a fresh beer, went to the living room and sprawled on the couch, stacking my feet on the coffee table and punching my way through the channels. In a minute I heard RV pad down the hallway to the bathroom, heard her tap on the door and say, "Can I come in?" then heard the door open and close.

Watching the channels change in front of me, watching the junk on the television, I was thinking about going back to the casino, about getting money on the credit cards and trying again. On the screen, a loaf of bread was talking to a wiener and a bottle of mustard. The wiener was up on end. The mustard bottle was flipping its cap around.

The bathroom door opened and closed again, and RV came into the living room. She stood at the door, looking at the television. "What are you watching?"

"Talking food," I said.

"Yeah, sure," she said. Frank clicked into the room behind her, smelled the edges of the rug, and then sprawled on the hardwood floor as if posing for a Great Dogs in History headstone.

"Sorry we didn't get back earlier," I said.

"I don't care," RV said. "I was fine. That's what Mom said. What do you guys think, I can't stay here alone?"

"What did you do?"

"Talked on the telephone," RV said. "I talked to Mallory and Skylar and Norby."

"Who's Skylar?" I said.

"Mallory's boyfriend," RV said. "But I think they're breaking up. They're not getting along anymore. They've been together three weeks."

"And who's Norby again?" I said.

"Why can't you remember any of my friends?"

"It's because you've got so many."

"Yeah, yeah," she said, showing me a palm, wiggling fingers. "I'm the most popular girl. Everybody loves me. I've got a lot of friends. I'm really wonderful." She made a goon face as if to say what she thought of that.

"Well, it's pretty much true," I said.

"Change the channel, will you?"

I flipped through the channels quickly until I got to MTV. She said, "Quick, turn this up. Turn this up. I love this song." Just as I knew she would.

I cranked the volume and watched her do the words with the singer. In a second she was singing in a whispery voice, the same way she did all the TV commercials. At first that surprised me. I couldn't figure why she would learn the commercials. When I asked, she said, "I don't know. They're there. I hear them all the time." It wasn't the big advertisers and tag lines she remembered, it was everything — voice-over, dialogue, sales pitch, music, jingles. Sometimes she even couch-acted the parts.

"So how much did you people lose?" she said, quitting the song and turning to me.

"I don't know. Ask your mother," I said.

"Ask your mother," RV said.

"Well, I don't know. It was too much."

"I already asked her," RV said.

"What'd she say?"

"She said it was for her to know and for me to find out. I said yeah, really." RV tugged at the TV remote. "You guys are gambling all the time, you know. Norby's father lost all their money gambling. That's why her mother got a divorce."

"We're not getting divorces in this family," I said.

"Well, you never know. But I'm not talking about that, I'm talking about you people going to those stupid casinos all the time. It's addictive. My biology teacher said it's very addictive."

"Isn't it time for you to go to bed?"

She made a frog face, her eyes goggled, her mouth drawn up in a clown smile, and did a goofy shrug. "Isn't it always?"

Three days later, Norby, Mallory, and RV spent the afternoon in RV's room talking about Mallory's breakup with Skylar.

I was taking another afternoon off, since there wasn't any reason not to, and I was making a special effort to memorize Norby. Mallory was fat and saccharine and who-could-forget-her evil, so she was easy. Norby had a pageboy and a scar on her forehead over her right eye, and I was sure I'd forget her in minutes. I sat in the living room reading a new issue of an Italian architectural magazine I'd been fond of since college. It was filled with buildings of a kind I'd never get a chance to build, dramatic and adventurous, full of exotic furniture, rich colors, delightful fabrics, all decidedly rare, not the sort of thing an architect did in Biloxi, or anywhere else very much, for that matter. When Jewel and I talked about building a house for ourselves, I thought I might have a chance to design the kind of house I would like to have, the kind of house that might appear in this magazine or some other like it. High ceilings, floods of light and color, curious rooms that made not much sense but were wonderful anyway, large open spaces for the main living areas. I'd wanted a tree-house room forever, some closet-size study on the third or even fourth floor, the only room up there in the middle of the trees, with a small drafting table and a chair and a few things. Jewel wanted a kitchen with a sitting room open to the outdoors. We had a lot of ideas for this house, but whenever I drew it up the place looked remarkably unexotic. Jewel studied the sketches and made encouraging noises, but I could tell how disappointed she was that I'd turned our fabulous ideas into a Mr. Dull house. So I stopped drawing it. It's best not to worry about what you can't do, about how talented you are not. It isn't useful. It isn't smart. If the time came to build a house, I would do something sufficient. Less than marvelous and transcendent, but with a little luck, pleasant. That would have to satisfy.

RV stuck her head out her bedroom door and asked if she could go to the video store with Mallory and Norby.

"What do you mean? Do you want me to take you?"

RV cleared her throat melodramatically. "Have you looked outside? Mallory's got her car."

"Mallory's only fourteen," I said.

"Is not," RV said. "She's fifteen and she got a car for her birthday."

I looked over my shoulder, and, sure enough, there was a brand-new car in the driveway. A Honda coupe. "I don't know," I said. "Does your mother let you ride with Mallory?"

"Sure," she said.

"RV?" I said, looking skeptical.

"We haven't discussed it," RV said.

"How long has she been driving?" I said.

"I don't know, long time, two weeks maybe," RV said. "Can we go?"

"Two weeks," I said. "Swell. Will you be gone long? Is that all you're doing, the video store and come right back?"

RV stamped her foot and put her fists on her hips. "Yes," she said, dragging the word out.

I looked at my watch. "Half an hour."

"An hour," RV said.

"To go to the video store?"

"O.K., forty-five minutes." She ducked into her room, shutting the door behind her. A moment later she opened the door wide and all three girls came out, headed for the front door.

"Hey," I said. "Mallory —" I gave her what I imagined was a stern look. "Let's be careful out there."

"Yes, sir," Mallory said. "I will. I'm always careful."

"Be especially careful today."

"Yes, sir," Mallory said.

"Bye, Daddy Ray," Norby said.

"Goodbye, dear," I said. I did not look but listened as the girls went out the door and down the walk. I listened to them getting in the car, giggling, listened to the car start and back slowly out of the drive, the tires crunching on the concrete. I listened to them shoot off toward Highway 90.

I shut my eyes and thought I would talk to Jewel about this. Hadn't Mrs. Miles driven the girls to church just weeks ago? Why was anybody driving at fifteen? Why would anybody give a daughter a car on her fifteenth birthday? Did this mean that RV would be driving when she was fifteen? Did we have to give RV a car? A fifteen-year-old was going to run a car into a tree, wasn't she? So what was the point in giving her a brand-new car? Airbags?

By the middle of October we'd dropped four thousand dollars on our new hobby. We had plenty of credit cards between us, so getting the advances wasn't a problem, but we were paying minimums due, so the balances weren't going anywhere. I spent Thursday night at the Paradise, playing blackjack, and came in at nine Friday morning and went to bed. When I woke up Jewel was there with me. It was raining, afternoon, and overcast, so it was quite dark in the room. She was reading by the light of the bedside lamp. I lay there and listened to the turning of tissue-thin pages for a few minutes, then I asked what it was she was reading.

"A thing by Dostoyevsky," she said.

"Oh yeah? What?"

"A novel called *The Gambler.* I read it in college. This is one of my college English textbooks." She held the book up with two hands. The type was tiny, and there were two columns per page. I remembered how efficient college textbooks were. This one looked as if it had never been touched.

I strained to see past the book, to the clock. It was nearly five. "Why aren't you reading Stanford Wong or Bryce Carlson or somebody?"

"Been there," she said. "Apparently Dostoyevsky was a big gambler. I thought there might be something here that would help."

"Nothing there will help." I rubbed my eyes, looking out the window at the rain-smeared dusk.

"Did you read it?" she said.

"No. It's got all those Russian names. Who can say them? You're reading along and all of a sudden, Unpronounceable appears. It's annoying. They should just change all the names to Wally and Jerome."

"So far, what I figure is you're kind of obsessed with gambling."

"Wait a minute," I said. "Look who's talking. The girl who came to the party with a tree." Frank came in and jumped up on the bed. The three of us listened to the rain.

"O.K., so *we're* obsessed. You know how much we've lost?"

"It'll come back," I said. "Some way. You'll waltz in and slip a dollar in a machine and hit triple diamonds. Ten thousand. That's the way it works — money takes a trip, money comes home."

"Unless it doesn't," Jewel said.

"Read *das* book," I said.

"Dinner," she said, getting off the bed. "Now that you're up I'm calling the Chinese place. What do you want?"

We ordered four dishes, more than we would eat, and Jewel left to pick up some things at the grocery, then swing by and get the food.

I got her novel and rooted around in it, trying to figure out which of the characters she thought I was like, which wasn't so hard, and to see if there were any tips in there that would help me play better. There weren't. There were a lot of Russians, and others, going about their business, and most of the names were easy to pronounce. There were some great speeches toward the end, but my review concluded that while the drama was charming, the author would have been better off with more gambling and less society.

I reflected on this while bathing.

I felt shitty about the money we'd lost, but I thought we might win it back, sooner or later. I was tired of trying to understand the attraction — Jewel said it was like drugs, same thing, but I wasn't sure. There were many pleasures, and it didn't seem to matter that much whether you won or lost. I sort of felt it was more exhilarating to lose a lot than win a little. Losing meant you had to play more, try harder. Losing burned intensely; winning became tepid fast.

The first time I hit something big on the slots, I hit three wild cherries, any position, on a dollar machine. I was excited for a few minutes, and sat staring at the three cherries, tapping the glass. That was riveting. It was four in the morning and I'd put a hundred-dollar bill in a dollar machine and hit the cherries right off — the cherries paid even if the symbols weren't on the payline. The machine made a special noise, the tighter, faster dinging that Jewel had talked about, and the light on top blinked, signaling the slot people. I sat in front of the machine and touched the symbols, one after another, repeatedly, in a blissful state.

Then I realized that if the cherries had been on the payline, the jackpot would've been huge, and that dimmed my enthusiasm.

After that we spent a lot of time comparing payoffs for different machines, trying to see which machine it was most profitable to play. I tried the hundred-dollar slots a couple of times, because I'd seen two old guys at the Paradise play them and win. They were nice guys with huge wads of hundred-dollar bills, softball-size wads. One guy owned a shipyard. The other guy was gay. I watched the gay guy win a hundred thousand one night. He just kept hitting. Got a sixty-thousand-dollar win, a sixteen, some others. The casino gave him his own personal uniformed security guard. I wanted him to give me lessons.

RV was spending the night at Mallory's, so she wasn't home when Jewel came back with the food around six. We ate and talked about going back to the casino. I wanted to go. She wasn't so sure.

"I'm trying the slots again," I said. "I need to give them another chance."

"You're giving away five percent," she said. "It's a sure loss."

"What are you talking about? You hit five grand on the slots, didn't you? Do it again and we're even."

"Sure, if we leave," Jewel said.

"How hard can that be?"

"It's been hard enough. What's changed? What makes you think, even if you got lucky and hit it, that you'd get out?"

"It's a plan. We go in with a plan," I said. Frank was next to the dining table, whimpering. Without thinking, I gave him a couple pieces of Mongolian beef.

Jewel sighed and dropped her head into her hands. "Please, Ray. Don't encourage him. We don't feed the dog at the table. Feed him at the table and he's going to beg every time we sit down. He's going sit there and whine."

"So?"

"Just don't," she said.

I gave Frank a stern look and pointed toward the living room. "Go on. Go sit on the couch. Go. Watch TV."

He twisted his head for a look, but didn't move.

"O.K.," I said to Jewel. "Here's what I want to do. Let's take a thousand and try the twenty-five-dollar slots. One thousand, that's it. We lose, we leave. How about it?"

"I don't care," Jewel said. "If that's what you want to do, do it."

"You don't want to go?"

"What does it matter? You're going anyway, aren't you?"

"Hey," I said. "You're the slot queen."

"I'm quitting, Ray," she said.

"Sure you are," I said.

"What's the chance it'll work, anyway? You've got forty shots."

"Sounds like a lot," I said.

"What if we hit something small, not five, but two. We quit then?"

"Up to you." I peeled a chunk of smoked tea duck off the bone, dipped it in the sauce. "Whatever way you want to go," I said, eating the duck.

Jewel stared for a second, then shook her head and began folding the tops of the food boxes, sticking the white cardboard tongues in their matching slits.

I came home at seven Saturday morning, leaving Jewel at the Paradise. I was going to shower and change clothes, but when I got to the house I found Mr. Miles, Mallory's father, on the front porch knocking on the door. He had an arm around RV's shoulder, and the wretched Mallory was in the car. As far as I knew there wasn't any plan about a seven A.M. return.

I hadn't met Mr. Miles, though I'd talked with him on the phone. RV was wearing yesterday's clothes and looked as if she hadn't slept.

I pulled the car into the yard so it wouldn't block Miles's exit. Somebody had gifted us with a big, crumpled McDonald's bag and a pair of soft-drink cups in the night.

"Early bird, eh?" Mr. Miles said, coming off the porch with RV in tow.

"Yeah. Left my wallet," I said. "I was going to get some fresh cinnamon rolls for breakfast. How are you, sir?" I introduced myself and shook hands with Miles, who patted RV's shoulder, then took his arm off her. She sat down on the porch steps.

"I guess there's a problem, or else you wouldn't be here this early?" I rubbed at my eyes, thinking this might reinforce the impression that I had just gotten up.

"Afraid so," he said. "Not a big problem. I mean, everybody's safe, everything's fine, but I thought I'd better bring RV home anyway."

"What happened?" I said.

"Well, the girls decided to go visit some boys this morning," he said. "And they forgot to tell us."

"At seven o'clock in the morning?" I said, looking from him to RV.

"More like five-thirty, quarter of six," he said. "I think they were up all night and then the boys called, and they went to visit out there at the Motel 6."

"Oh good," I said. "Motel 6." I leaned down for a look at RV, but she dodged her head away, staring at the bushes.

"They were at the house all night, but went out the window this morning, far as we can figure."

"Got it," I said. I didn't really get it, but I didn't want him to know that. "Well, thanks for bringing her home, now, uh, you went to get her there at the motel?"

"Yes," he said. "It's a mixed-up story. There was another girl who came by our house to get her car, but she was locked out and came to the door and woke us, and that's when we found out where the girls were."

"I see. Two girls spent the night and then went to the motel. One came back. That's when you found out."

"Right," Mr. Miles said. "I went out there, knocked on the

door. Mallory and RV were in one of the beds. The boys were on the other side of the room. They were watching cartoons on television."

"Mallory and RV were in bed?" I said.

Mr. Miles nodded. "It was a room with two beds. One was still made, and the girls were in the other. The boys were sitting on the bed that was made, as far as I could tell."

"O.K.," I said, looking at the car, then back to Mr. Miles. "They were *in* the bed?"

"Yes. But dressed and everything. I didn't see them get out, but they came right outside. I told the boys get out of the room, and then RV and Mallory followed."

"You didn't see them get out of the bed?"

"No, I didn't," Mr. Miles said. There was an ugly lull in the conversation, and then he said, "They were watching cartoons."

I bent over and looked at my shoes, pushed my hair around for a second. "Mrs. Miles was in the car this whole time?"

"Right. Downstairs in the car."

"Good. I see." I backed away a few feet, giving him a clear shot at the porch steps. "Well, thanks very much for everything, for bringing RV. I'm sorry. They're kind of hard to handle at this age, aren't they?"

"Yep," he said.

"They can be trouble." I reached down to mess with RV's hair but she tilted her head out of reach.

"Yep," Mr. Miles said. He stood for a moment in the yard, looking over at his car, then turned back to me. "I feel really bad about this. We feel responsible since she was staying at our house —"

"Oh no," I said. "They'll go out any open window."

He smiled and looked relieved. "I guess," he said. "Well, I'll be going."

He stepped back up so we could shake hands again, then

made it to the driveway, got into his black car, backed out. I watched him go, then turned to RV.

"O.K. What's the story with this?"

"No story. What?" RV said.

"You were at a motel?" I said.

"We were visiting Robbie and Skylar," she said. "We were watching cartoons. What's the matter with that?"

"Motel 6?"

"They're just friends. I don't know why everybody's got their panties in a wad. Mallory's dad was screaming at her all the way home."

"She isn't supposed to be going to Motel 6 to meet up with her boyfriend."

"They broke up. Remember? I told you."

"I remember," I said. "So, like, rehearse this for me — you went over there this morning. Is this something you planned?"

"No. They called," RV said.

"They called Mallory's house?"

"Well, Mallory called first, and they called back."

"At five-thirty?"

"Yeah. We were with them last night at a party at Casey's house. Then we went to Mallory's at midnight, and they called from the motel, and we talked on the phone for a long time. Like, until three. Then Mallory and me and Bridget sort of stayed up, and then we sort of slept, but we didn't really really sleep."

"And at five Mallory called Skylar and you went over there?"

"Yeah, he came and got us," RV said.

"You and Mallory and Bridget? I've never even heard of Bridget. Who's Bridget?"

"Friend of Mallory's," RV said. "It's so bright out here." She lifted her jacket and put the collar over her head, the way a boxer coming into the ring might wear a towel. There was a weird opening where her face was. I couldn't see much of her face in such deep shadow, but she had kind of a Pietà look.

"Take that off your head," I said.

"No. It's too bright. Can we go in? Are there any tacos or tostados or anything in the kitchen?"

"I don't know what's in the kitchen," I said. "Haven't you eaten?"

"I'm not hungry. Forget I asked."

"I'll make you something."

"No. I want to rest. I'm tired. I didn't get any sleep, remember? Are you just coming home?"

"Yes." I unlocked the front door and let her into the house. Frank came out of the bedroom fast, skidding on the hardwood floor as he turned for the door.

RV pulled the jacket off her head. "You gambled all night long? I don't know why you're yelling at me. You stay out all night gambling."

"I'm not yelling," I said.

"Are too," she said.

"You can yell at me later."

She slumped onto the couch, pulling Frank after her, hugging him. "You're not grounding me, are you?"

"I don't know. We have to wait for your mother."

"There's a thing," RV said.

"What kind of a thing?"

"Like a party. Tonight," RV said. "Everybody's meeting at Bridget's house. She's got a pool. Everybody's going to sit around and talk. Everybody goes there now. I'm supposed to go."

"It's just a guess, but I'll bet you're going to stay home tonight. Have a night on earth, here with your parents."

"Parent," RV said.

"Whatever," I said.

RV microwaved some Chinese food and took that and a tall glass of pale blue fruit drink to her room. I tried to get Jewel at the Paradise but she didn't answer the page. I took a shower, then tried again. Still no answer. I looked in on RV. She'd fallen asleep with all her clothes on. I took the bowl she'd had the Chinese in and put it in the kitchen sink. Then I went to our bedroom and lay on the bedspread, resting. I must've fallen asleep. I woke up at nine-thirty when Jewel called from the Paradise. I heard the slots banging in the background.

"Hi," she said. "Where are you? I thought you were coming back."

"I got here and Mallory's father was here with RV," I said. "He rescued her from Motel 6. She and Mallory were out there with some boys."

"What?" Jewel said.

"RV was in the motel room with Skylar and somebody else. I don't know. This is your turf."

"What are you talking about?" she said.

"Listen," I said. "RV and Mallory went to Motel 6 at around five-thirty this morning to meet some boys, one of whom was Mallory's boyfriend, or ex-boyfriend. They were watching cartoons out there. Mr. Miles found out about it, went and got them, brought RV back here at seven. They were on the porch when I drove up."

"Oh, Jesus," Jewel said.

"Why don't you jump a cab, or I'll come get you, and we can try to deal with this," I said.

"What's RV doing?"

"Sleeping," I said. "She was earlier. I paged you at seven-thirty."

"They comped me a room after you left. I was going to go back and finish playing," she said.

"You played all night."

"I know," she said. "It's terrible."

"Where are we?"

"I don't know. How did you end up?"

"Even," I said.

"Well I had a good run, then I went in the tank. I lost pretty good."

"Last night you were quitting."

"Don't start, please, Ray," she said. "Uh, I need to play. I can get back if I play."

"How much did you lose?"

"Thousand, maybe more," she said. "You're sure you left even?"

"Yeah," I said. "For last night. I lost Thursday."

"What day is it now?" she said.

"Saturday." I curled the telephone cord around my finger waiting for her to say something. When she didn't, I said, "I think you were right. We've got to do something."

"I'm getting the hang of it," she said.

"What's the evidence of that?"

"Jesus, what a jerk. If you were here and I was there, you'd tell me to get screwed. I'm trying to win, O.K.? It's worth the risk. I'll be back by noon. She's not getting up before noon, is she?"

"I don't know."

"Ray?" she said. "Ray? You there?"

"Sure," I said. "You're right. Good luck."

"I love you," she said.

"Me, too," I said. "I've got this covered, don't worry. She wants to go out tonight but I told her she couldn't. She's going to want your authority on that."

"Do it on yours," Jewel said. "O.K.? I'll be there when I get there."

Late Saturday afternoon I was in the front yard working on Frank's coat with a special saw-like comb that was supposed to strip away the dead hair and thin the coat when Jewel pulled up in a Yellow Cab. She paid the cabbie and walked across the yard looking worn down. I gave her a kiss. "You're beat," I said.

"Yes sir," she said.

"Do all right?"

"I wouldn't say that, no," she said. "Where's the delinquent daughter?"

"Inside with the delightful Mallory. She rushed over to commiserate because RV can't go tonight."

At that moment RV and Mallory came out of the house. "Hi, Mom," RV said. "What are you doing?"

"Hi, baby," Jewel said. "I'm going to make some coffee, clean some stuff, and then I'm going to make dinner."

"Can I talk to you for a minute?"

"Sure. What about?"

"I don't know, I just want to talk," RV said. "You know. I'll go in with you."

"I'll stay here," Mallory said, sitting in the rocking chair on the porch. There was a swing there, too.

RV followed Jewel inside. I kept working on Frank. Mallory rocked and watched the street. I caught her practicing her silly grin a couple of times. In two minutes RV yanked open the front door and came outside, stomping across the wood-plank porch to sit with Mallory.

"Should we go somewhere where we can talk?" Mallory whispered.

RV did an elaborate sigh. "It doesn't matter. They're not letting me go anywhere." She looked at me and made a face.

"I may not go either," Mallory said. "There's nobody there I need to see. Skylar's not going. He is so great. Sometimes I can't believe he still likes me."

"I wouldn't like you," RV said. "Not if you dumped on me the way you dumped on him."

"Never did," Mallory said.

"Oh yeah?" RV said. "Like that time with Malcolm was nothing?"

"We went for a walk," Mallory said.

RV held a hand up by her ear, wiggling her fingers. "Talk to it," she said.

"Really," Mallory said.

"At least your parents trust you," RV said. "At least you have parents."

Mallory glanced at me, then dropped her voice to a whisper and said something I couldn't hear.

RV was peeling the sole off her sandal by dragging it toe-first across the porch floor. "They're all like that. They lose it."

"Really," Mallory said. "What about you and Jeff?"

"Not," RV said.

"Bridget says he likes you. She talked to him."

"When?" RV said.

"Today. She called before I came over," Mallory said.

"Why didn't she tell me?" RV said.

"She thinks you're mad about this morning. Besides, it wasn't a big deal. She just said it."

"He's all right," RV said. She watched me gather up the hair that had come off Frank when I was raking him.

I went up the steps onto the porch, smiled at Mallory, bent to give RV a kiss on the head. She tried to duck away but I caught her. "How's my party girl?"

"How's Bub the Gambler?"

I opened the front door and let Frank go in. "I would be better if you hadn't been in the motel this morning."

"Oh, God. It was nothing. We were over there watching cartoons with some guys — Skylar and Jeff and some other guys. It's so stupid. That kind of stuff is all you ever think about, you and Mom."

I squinted at her and at Mallory. "Well?" I said.

RV rolled her eyes and at the same time made a crazy finger, circling the side of her head.

"C'mon, RV. A motel? You know better."

"It was nothing. Just leave us alone, O.K.?" She got out of the swing and signaled Mallory. "Let's take a driveway ride."

"Sorry," I said. "I was just playing."

"Yeah, I know," RV said. "We're just sitting out here listening to tapes." They were halfway to Mallory's car when RV stopped. "Did you at least win?"

"Ask your mom," I said.

"I did. She didn't answer."

"Big winners," I said. "Monster. We're going to own the place in a week."

Jewel was at the sink washing dishes. I crossed the living and dining rooms into the kitchen, kissed her cheek, which was all she offered, put Frank's hair in the trash and his raking comb on the rack in the closet, then sat on the green stool with the straw seat. Jewel was sudsing up the parts of the Cuisinart.

"Glad you could make it, Ramone," Jewel said.

"You've got that good smoky smell," I said.

"Yeah, I know." She sniffed the sleeve of her blouse. "You've calmed down."

"Yeah, I've calmed down. Was I uncalm earlier?"

"I don't believe I did this," she said.

"Quit worrying about it. It's fine."

"Wait until you've heard the numbers." She smiled at me in an awkward way.

"Be a man to whom numbers mean nothing, is what my old

pap told me," I said. "You were a thousand down, I figure it's maybe three now." I watched her, trying to see if I was close.

"That's the area all right."

"It doesn't matter," I said, pushing my hair back a couple of times with both hands. "Could be fifty."

"I don't know why I kept thinking I was going to get a run. Things broke my way a few hands, then the other way twice as many. I pulled my bets down, but when things turned I couldn't get up fast enough."

"I thought you were going to stick with the slots?"

"No," she said. "I've got all this strategy down, I ought to be able to do better."

"Law of large numbers," I said.

"What?"

"I read about the law of large numbers. You have to play thousands of hands to win. Some guys go two or three years without winning. It's in one of the books."

"At this rate we can't afford years."

"It's going to turn," I said. "Why don't you get out of those clothes. We'll wash the washables, put the others in the car for the cleaners."

Jewel pulled ATM slips and Paradise receipts out of her pockets, a tin of aspirin, a toothbrush. She went into the laundry room and stripped down to her panties, dumping her clothes into the washer. "I'm taking a bath," she said.

"Good idea," I said, pointing to the sink. "I'll finish up here and run the washer."

"I talked to RV," she said. "She's O.K. She didn't even ask about tonight. I mean, she said that you'd said no, but she didn't ask me if she could go."

"Well she stomped out onto the porch a minute ago," I said.

"Oh," Jewel said, drawing her head back. "On this motel deal, is there some something I'm missing?"

"I don't know. She and Mallory were in one of the beds

and the boys were across the room. That's what Miles said."

"In bed?" Jewel said. "Did you tell me that?"

"I don't remember. But they're not doing sex with six guys in the room at their age, right? We didn't even have sex with six people in our heyday."

"Maybe you didn't," Jewel said.

"Funny. Good one," I said.

"I don't want to think about this part," Jewel said. "Her and those boys, needing them. I'm dreading this. I remember. You want them so bad, just a look, a smile, anything. Some talk. I hate for her to feel that. Gives me chills."

"Maybe it doesn't happen that way now," I said.

"Don't be dumb. It's always that way."

I caught her and ran my open hand across her bare shoulder. She hugged me, put her face into my neck, pressed herself against me.

Then she pulled away suddenly. "Jesus, even my hair smells like smoke." She backed toward the door leading to the bathroom hallway. "Give me fifteen minutes," she said. "I'll be clean as a whistle."

Jewel got a nap, then we ate hamburgers she cooked on the stove, and then we watched television all night, the three of us together. We watched a mystery movie RV and I rented from the video store, and then another one on HBO. There was a thunderstorm. Frank curled up on the rug in front of us, and then on the couch beside RV. It was a perfect night. Even RV seemed to like it. What I wondered, and what Jewel and I talked about before we fell asleep later, was why there weren't more nights like that, when we were a family, when all of us felt comfortable in our roles, when nothing more than each other's company was necessary. We didn't have any answers, but we both knew that night was something to be cherished.

A little over a week later, on a Monday night, I talked to my father on the phone, went through the usual routine with him, the catalog of his ailments, the complaints about the woman who was coming in every day to help him out, the problem he was having with his testicles, how they were raw because he spent all his time sitting and he never moved much. I made some joke about that and he laughed and made some other joke himself, laughed at that, too, so altogether it was a better conversation than usual.

Then Tuesday morning the nurse from the service called and said, "There's been some trouble with your father." I figured he was sick or something, maybe he had to go to the hospital, but then the woman said she had come in that morning and found him tangled up on the floor, his knee cocked through the scissors-like legs of an overturned TV tray. And then she said my father had died.

"He died?" I said.

She repeated the explanation and then gave the telephone to a policeman who said he was there overseeing things, and wanted to know if I had a preference for funeral arrangements. I didn't. I gave him the name of the only funeral home I knew, some family-run Catholic place I remembered because I'd been to grade school with one of the children. I asked to speak to the nurse again.

"He went peaceful, Mr. Ray," she said. "He was comfortable. I prayed for him."

"I thought he was twisted up in a TV tray," I said.

"Well, he was. But he was O.K. after that, and then he went to rest, and when I went back he wasn't breathing."

"So he was alive when you got in this morning?"

"Yes," the woman said. "He couldn't answer the door because he was caught in that table thing, but once we got the security people and got inside, we put him on the bed and he seemed to be fine. He was very peaceful then, very relaxed and comfortable. The television was on. He was trying to watch a tape, I think, but it wasn't running."

"After you put him on the bed, you mean?"

"No, before. That's what he'd been doing, trying to set up that *Sound of Music* tape he liked."

"That's when he got caught in the TV tray?"

"I think so, yes," she said.

We went through it again, and then I said I'd be driving over the following day and I asked her to tell the complex manager to leave a key for me.

As soon as I got off the phone I called my mother.

Telling her wasn't hard because she seemed to know what I was going to say from my tone of voice. When I heard her crying on the other end of the line I felt stupid for having called her instead of driving across town to tell her in person, but as soon as I said something about coming over, she said, "That's not necessary. I'm fine." And her crying stopped.

"I thought I'd go over there tomorrow," I said.

"Fine," she said. "I'm coming with you."

"I know," I said. "Do you want to stay over here tonight? I could come get you now, and then we'll go when we get up."

"What? No," she said. "What is it, an eight-hour drive? Get me in the morning. That'll be fine. And give me the woman's name, the one you talked to."

Wednesday morning was crisp and chilly, a dry cold. Highway 10 wasn't crowded. The speed limit was seventy, so I drove just under eighty. Mother wasn't crying, but her eyes were ringed and puffy.

"I'm not looking at the body," she said as we passed Hammond, Louisiana. "They'll ask us, and I'm going to say no. You can if you want to, but I think it's ghoulish. You don't think that's terrible, do you?"

"No," I said. "It makes sense."

"Some people want to see. They want to spit in the eye of death, but not me. I can't do anything for him now. I had my chance."

"You did plenty, Mom," I said.

"Maybe. I don't know. I shouldn't have left him there alone, that's what it is, really. That's what I think. I should have made him move, or stayed there with him, either one."

"He could've come," I said, trying to remember the last time I'd seen my father — it must have been the summer after she moved. I remember thinking he wanted to be coaxed. We did some of that, but not enough to get the job done.

"I think I discouraged him," she said.

"No, you didn't. You begged him to come."

"It doesn't do any good to lie about it, Ray."

"I'm not lying," I said. "I'm just trying to remember. You wanted him to move, and sort of reluctantly did yourself after he said he wouldn't. Besides, you were supposed to get things straightened away, weren't you?"

"It shocked me when he didn't come," Mother said. "I was sure he would. That hurt."

"He was going to," I said. "He talked about it all the time. He missed you so much, but he couldn't get off the dime."

"I missed him."

"I was thinking about how he smelled," I said. "Like if you threw his shirts in the laundry with yours, you got that scent of him? Sometimes I think I smell like that now. The sheets I sleep on or something."

She said, "I hate when people die. When I die, just dump me out the door, will you? Put me in a Hefty Lawn and Leaf sack and drag me to the curb." She stared out the window of my Explorer. "What would he think if he saw us speeding over there right now?"

"He'd think it was fine," I said.

"No," she said. "You know better than that. He'd think it was a waste of gasoline, he wouldn't like it."

"He'd say that, but he'd want us coming."

"He had a hard time being ordinary, Hopper did. Never quite made it up to that. You're taking right after him."

I shook my head and locked the cruise control at seventy-eight. I didn't want to take care of my father. I was nervous, as if the bad news wasn't at hand, but was still out there. As if we were driving to Houston for further medical tests to uncover my mother's lung cancer or heart disease. When things were quiet in the car, the thought "My father's dead" rang over and over in my head until the phrase was like an echo. Then, when I was able to forget for a few miles, I'd suddenly realize I was thinking about something I wanted to tell him when we got to Houston.

I hadn't suspected that he was about to die, but now that it had happened, I was sure I'd known. It was obvious from the complaints, the nursing service, the difficulty he had keeping track of his pills, the way he sometimes seemed out of his head if my phone call caught him after a nap.

When Jewel's sister was killed in the car crash, it didn't feel like anything. We were friends and it was nothing, like she'd been erased. The police woke us at three in the morning and I was all business. Up and dressed and getting Jewel going and heading for the hospital and then making the arrangements. I thought it ought to feel worse, but it only felt like stuff to do. So I took care of things. I thought I'd cry later, but never did. Weeks went by, months. I didn't miss Jewel's sister. What was different was that I didn't talk to her the way I had, didn't sit down with her and chat. Otherwise things were the same. She vanished. It didn't matter.

The same thing was going to happen with my father. I wanted to do it right, to feel sad, but I didn't. I felt taut and tired, and I had to drive all the way to Houston. Some inevitable thing had happened. I didn't want to mess with funeral directors and cemetery guys. I didn't want to smile and act lost and accept their condolences. I didn't want to nod and be nodded at, knowingly, when I was already looking forward to having it done with, being finished with him.

I might miss the telephone calls, his gravelly voice and the endless litany of small troubles — bowels, bankers, difficulty seeing and walking, bad food, the nurse who spoke no English — the complaints about everything and everyone, leavened occasionally with a recognition that he was being self-indulgent. And I would miss the hesitant questions about my mother — how was she, why did she not call him more often, did I think she still loved him at all? That was the part of him I loved most.

Mother stirred in the seat next to me. "Stop at the next rest station," she said. "I need to stop. O.K.? Have you got any Kleenex in this car? And what is this about you people losing money at the casino? Jewel said five thousand dollars."

"We've lost a bunch," I said.

"Is it that much?"

"Yes, maybe more. We didn't exactly keep track."

"So. Up jumps the devil," she said. "Are you having some kind of problem? Is the marriage O.K.? What is it?"

She looked out her window as a bright chrome eighteen-wheel tanker truck passed, distorting the reflection of the Explorer in its curved side.

"We're fine," I said.

She waved me off. "Never mind, don't tell me another thing about it, I don't want to hear. Whatever it is, it'll make perfect sense to you and no sense at all to me. Can you afford to lose that much money?" She tapped the window, pointing at a rest stop we were passing, a place with concrete pavilions and a glass-enclosed visitors' center. "Hey," she said.

My father had turned the downstairs of the condo into a private nursing home — a single bed, a chest of drawers, a chair, a TV, the dining table, a collection of plastic containers, a carton of Depends, a box for his pill bottles. He had the living room furniture piled up in the dining room. It was pitiful. My mother sniffled and crunched a tissue, and I stared at the room. Someone had cleaned things up after my father's death. There were sheets and pillowcases folded neatly on the end of the bed. The magazines were all straightened, as were the books in the single row alongside the bed. The dishes were clean. Everything was put away. There was a note from the nursing-service woman, in a childlike scrawl, repeating the story of how tranquil my father had been at the moment of death. His wallet was in the middle of a dining table cluttered with bills, letters, manila folders, unopened mail, small tools, two boxes of ballpoint pens.

Mother said, "This is not what I want to see."

We sat in the chairs in the converted living room and had drinks. We didn't talk, just sat and absorbed the situation, drank, rested from the drive.

When her drink was half gone, she said, "This is something, isn't it?"

"It looks pretty bleak, all right."

"He died right here." She waved at the TV tray, which was back in its place alongside his favorite chair. "Do you feel that eerie thing? Like his presence? I don't know. He's not coming back, is he? He wasn't such a bad guy. He was difficult, but that's O.K. for a man to be. Better that than too easy. It wasn't much fun when he was on your case, though."

"I think he meant well," I said. "He never meant anything but well."

"That's the truth. We'll put that on the headstone," she said.

My shoulders hurt. In the room it felt as though time had stopped moving, everything arrested, frozen, held that way. Nobody who had to do with us would ever move around in that condo again. It was a dead place we had to spend a couple of days. I felt the fact of my father's death. I wanted to sleep, to get out of there by whatever means. I said, "He was fine. He didn't deserve to die, though I guess that's stupid, who does? Last time I talked to him, he was telling me about a rash on his testicles."

"I think you can keep that to yourself," my mother said.

"Maybe I'll go upstairs and take a nap," I said. "Will that upset you? I'll think of something smarter to say afterwards."

"You don't have to think a thing," she said. "It's just worse than I anticipated."

"Don't think about it," I said. "I'm sorry, Mother." I got up and stood behind her chair, then wondered why I'd done that, wondered if it was because I'd seen it in a hundred movies, on a thousand TV shows. *The Comforting.* I put my hands on her, on her shoulders, on the sides of the tops of her arms, I stroked her hair, leaned down and kissed her cheek, seeing each of the gestures in my imagination before doing it. "It's O.K.," I whispered.

She reached up with her left hand and patted softly the side of my head. "Thank you, baby," she said.

There were three bedrooms upstairs. One was a guest bedroom that I had always used when I visited. It had twin beds, a TV, a night table with an electric clock on it. Some boxes of my father's business stuff were stuck in the corner. There was a walk-in closet. I stretched out on the bed, put a washcloth over my eyes, and folded my arms across my chest. The pillow was foam rubber, old, uncomfortable. I thought I remembered it from childhood, but that might have been wrong. It had a ridge that hit right at the base of my neck. I listened to my mother in the master bedroom across the hall, her old bedroom. She was opening drawers and closets, moving stuff around.

Then she knocked on my door. "Come in," I said.

She stepped into the small bedroom and sat on the edge of the second bed. "I know you think he was horrible to me," she said. "But I gave as good as I got most of the time. He was crazy, like he always thought he was right, always thought things should make sense, thought you could find a right way or a best way for things. But that was a luxury for me. Another reason to love him."

It was dark outside and the floodlamps from the adjacent condos shot in through the mini-blinds. Under the corner of the washcloth I saw stuff floating in the beams of light.

She said, "It could've been much worse. He was scared at the end. He had nowhere to go, nobody to turn to. What was he going to do? I think it made him feel better to take it out on me, order me around, say I was crazy."

"You are crazy, aren't you?" I lifted the washcloth off my eyes to squint at my mother.

She smiled in a way so faint that it barely disturbed her face.

Strips of shadow from the blinds crossed the ceiling and peeled down the walls of the small bedroom. Mother scooted up onto the other bed, straightened her skirt, wiggled her feet in their white canvas shoes. "Sure I am," she said. "And I don't want to go out there alone."

"There's a lot of work," I said.

"You know what? I was thinking we could call somebody and get it packed and shipped back without ever getting into it. We could get into it later."

I adjusted the washcloth and thought how wonderful that would be. It was as if suddenly we didn't have to have the surgery after all. I got a chill running my spine. "You think we can do that?"

"We're the boss," she said. "I'll store it at the house, or get a place."

"He wouldn't approve," I said. "Hopper would want lists, plans, details, diagrams. Research. The whole deal. Of course, now that he's dead, he doesn't want a thing."

"That'll do, Ray," she said.

"I was trying to help," I said.

"It'll be good. It's cleaner. We never have to see the body, they take care of everything, we don't have to tear it all down, we just call them and get it done."

I sighed. "Well, I like the idea."

"You know, when *my* father died it was a mess," she said. "He died in the house. Lots of boiling water, steam everywhere, heavy air, thick drawn curtains, constant scrubbing floors, washing bed linens and his bedclothes, relatives milling around, doctors coming and going."

"Dickens," I said.

"I can't imagine going through Hopper's clothes, choosing this and that," she said. "His things. We'll keep everything. I'll call Bekins tomorrow, we'll meet them and get it set up, and that'll be that."

Tension jetted out of my shoulders. I rolled my neck back and forth on the pillow. What a wonderful thought.

"I don't want to stay any longer than we have to," she said. "Although, I kind of wish he were here watching me."

"I was thinking what if he was on his way back from the doctor. And you two were going to watch a National Geographic special, *The Big Cats,* at ear-snapping volume. I used to come up here to hide from the noise when you watched TV."

"Wait till you can't hear," she said.

"He was kind of a freak on that volume."

"Who isn't a freak some way or other? For me he was like a guiding light, you know? God, I hate this." She got off the bed and split the blinds with two fingers. "Your father was good to me most of my life. You can't ask for more than that."

"You know, I guess."

"Yes," she said. "But I can't stand being here, it's making me nuts. I shouldn't have left him. That was wrong."

Jewel called late to find out how things were going. I got the phone downstairs and filled her in. "We're calling the movers and bailing out quick," I said. "That's what Mother wants to do. She feels guilty about his dying."

"Like she should have made him move or something?"

"Yeah. I didn't do much either."

"Like he really listened to you, Ray," Jewel said.

"I could've tried harder."

"So what's it like otherwise?" she asked.

"Nothing. Empty rooms, like we're waiting for somebody to come home. He turned the downstairs into a homemade hospital or something. It's awful."

"What's that mean?"

"He had everything pushed out of the way, only functional stuff around, pee pots everywhere — he was having some bladder problem, I guess. He was living in this one room down here, had a dresser, a TV, bath — like a hospital room."

"I'm sorry," she said. "So are you O.K.?"

"I'm tired. He's gone. Sometimes it seems like a joke and he'll show up any minute. Getting somebody else to handle everything is a relief. I guess we're doing stuff, I don't know."

"You want me to look for storage places?"

"Yeah, if you would. That'd be great. Out by Mother's. Is RV O.K.?"

"Boy trouble with Jeff," Jewel said.

"Oh yeah? Have we met Jeff?"

"No. And Randall got a Vespa, so she wants a Vespa."

"I thought they wanted cars."

"Randall already has a car. This is something to play with."

"I see," I said. "Who's Randall?"

"He's like, *there,* when she chills," Jewel said. "That's what I hear, anyway."

"Oh. Cool."

"What about the funeral?"

"We don't speak funeral," I said. "Cremate and hide the ashes. Nobody leaves the house. No service, no marker, no nothing. We'll be back there in two days."

"Well, that'll be good. Being back."

"I guess. There's something about him not being here," I said. "He can't scowl anymore. He can't dismiss you. I have this urge to poke into things, see what's what. I can move stuff with impunity."

"Hmm?" Jewel wasn't listening to me. She was carrying on a conversation on the side. Then she said, "RV wants a word with you."

I listened to the phone being passed. Then RV said, "Hey, Ray."

"How are you, doll?"

She sighed. "O.K., I guess. Randall's Vespa is really cool. It's real old. Maybe I'll steal it and take you for a ride sometime. I'm sorry about, you know — everything."

"Thank you, sweetie. I miss you."

"Yeah, me too. Nobody's ragging on me about my room, my homework, and my clothes."

"I love your room, homework, and clothes," I said. "I dream of them."

"You're a sick pigeon," she said. "Here, Mom. Your husband's being sick on the phone."

"Am not," I yelled into the handset.

"They're going to another party tonight," Jewel said when she came back on the line.

I was staring at the furniture in the living room, at the way my father had changed things to fit his new life.

"All this furniture is so still," I said. "It's a deathwatch."

"I'm sorry, Ray," she said.

"Thanks," I said. "I mean, talking to him on the phone he complained about everything, but seeing it firsthand is different."

"It's bad enough without feeling guilty," she said. "Forget that, will you?"

"Yeah, I know. Is there any other news?"

"One of the cards is over limit," she said. "The Chase card."

"Get another one. Bank of America. Bank of New York. First National. Supplies are endless."

"This is not a healthy attitude, Ray. Maybe we should go back to architecture."

"Can't," I said. "Coming into Houston, I realized that building is aggression. New parking garages, pint-size office buildings, freeways — they're all explosions in the center of otherwise entirely satisfactory settings. I don't know why I never saw it before."

"Maybe this isn't the time," she said.

"I haven't been working much for a while, anyway. Or hadn't you noticed?"

"I noticed. That's why I brought it up."

"We'll probably get something from the estate," I said. "That'll help. Not much, but we can pay some on the cards."

We said goodnight and I put the phone back in its charging cradle, then sat on the edge of my father's bed, looking at the living room from that vantage, trying to see it as he had. It looked as if everything in the room were leaning toward me just slightly, just enough to notice. In a few minutes I lay back on the bed and closed my eyes. I heard stuff outside — buzzing streetlights, cars coming and going, chirps of security systems set, footsteps on the walk, muffled young voices in animated conversation passing outside my father's door.

Mother had the knack. The next day people from the funeral home, the cemetery, the moving company, the condo rental agency, the Goodwill, the Sisters of Our Savior Mission, and several other helpful organizations started arriving at noon. They were fortyish men in smooth suits who got confused with all the papers they needed to get signed.

I sat at the dining table eating a sandwich I'd made from roast beef and white bread from the deli section of the local grocery. The guys doing the helping were constantly pointing at spots my mother was supposed to initial on their papers. They'd tap the signature lines with their Cross ballpoints. I scanned a brochure called "Finally, an Island of Rest" while the cemetery man, Steve Walker, a blond and too healthy guy in his late thirties, talked perpetual care, interment exclusions, monument privilege restrictions, lawn crypts, the merits of Urn Garden versus Columbarium Niche.

The funeral director brought an aluminum suitcase filled with photographs and color samples and swatches of coffin cloth. He was prepared no matter which way we wanted to go. The Bekins guy spent an hour going around the house touching things and making notes, while his associate put green numbered tags on all the furniture, lamps, appliances — anything that was to be packed individually. The Sisters of Our Savior representative was younger, dressed the way priests used to dress when they ventured off church grounds, only he looked like a skinhead, so either you couldn't take him seriously or you had to take him so seriously that it was scary.

Most of the people talked about death but looked as though they were more interested in beach volleyball and Eddie Bauer. Every man was practiced, efficient, helpful. Not one was unctuous, oily, lubricated, or waxy.

During a break in the action I said, "Whatever happened to stereotypes? This is quite a show you whomped up."

"Thank you," Mother said. "It's my 'Baked While You Sleep' background. We'll be gone tomorrow, day after at the latest."

"No wonder everybody loves you. When we get back I'm driving you around to look for that Larroquette guy you were so interested in. We're going everywhere. No stone unturned."

"We need a storage place. You can drive me around to look at storage places."

"Jewel's looking."

"She is? Good."

While waiting for the next visitor, she read the material left behind by the last one. She was still handsome. Her skin shined and her hair was salt-and-peppery, off the shoulder in a fifties way she'd worn since I could remember. There was something winsome about her, even in her sixties. I had a hard time thinking of her and my father together, meeting at college, dating, going out in Galveston, lingering along the boardwalk, or partying at Sui Jen, an ancient dance hall that teetered out over the water back then, until some hurricane got it in the mid-fifties. I'd seen photos of them in my father's 1953 Studebaker, waving at the camera, looking daffy, driving off from my grandparents' house. He was the drummer in a jazz quartet that played around, and my mother was never too far from the bandstand, smoking cigarettes and drinking her bourbon so slowly that the glass never seemed to change. Wearing black tailored suits with white piping. There were crazy parties — ones that ended in car games that nearly killed all participants, or in the good fun of hanging people upside down off the fourteenth-floor penthouse garden of the Milam Hotel up in Houston, or in gunshots over in the fourth ward. I had heard the stories as a kid, retold with fondness and delight over Sunday dinner, or when old friends who only showed up every couple of years came to visit. I knew my parents more from those stories and from photographs and eight-millimeter home movies than from memory. These were events or afternoons caught forever, showing me what it had been like. I couldn't pinpoint when the photographs and movies replaced my own real memories, and I had a few schematic recollections independent of the pictures — something at grade school with a lay teacher, a spanking I'd gotten for lying about some cookies, shooting arrows in the yard — but mostly my memory was snapshots. I'd see a photo of the house we lived in when I was ten and recognize the furniture without actually remembering it. I couldn't imagine what it was like to sit in that chair doing my homework, as I was in dozens of pictures, or to be on the kitchen cabinet talking to my mother, as I was in others, or to be playing with Christmas toys. I said I remembered, but what I meant was I remembered the pictures. Nothing in them had heft or dimension, they were all signs, images I could identify but not give life to.

"We were finally talking about him coming to Mississippi," my mother said. "Hopper wasn't ready, but he was getting closer. I mean, what was he going to do? Sixty-eight — a new romance? I thought he'd give in and move this year. If he didn't, I was going to come back here." She was swiveling my father's wallet in circles on the dining table. "I thought we'd visit a few times, then, gradually, you know . . ."

"He always asked me about you," I said. "How you were and everything."

"Who else did he know? Everybody else who lives here is thirty. Maybe the woman two doors down on the other side of the walk who used to bring the potato soup. He might have taken up with her, I guess. But she died a while ago."

My mother was staring out the sliding glass doors at the narrow patio overgrown with wisteria. Bees buzzed vigorously among the blue-violet flower clusters that hung off the vines. A Weber barbecue grill I bought them one summer was out there.

It wasn't as easy as Mother said it would be. She decided we had to go through Hopper's papers, the stuff in the backs of the closets, the china, the books, the family records, photographs, and the rest of it. I went to the U-Haul store to buy a few boxes and found this six-inch-wide green plastic wrap in a five-hundred-yard roll. The plastic stuck to itself, so you could wrap anything with it. It was like industrial-strength Saran Wrap on a handle. We spent a day or two sorting, boxing, wrapping, reducing my father's life to its simplest parts. And since he'd kept files for bills, insurance, Social Security, investments, medical expenses, and so on, the only thing left untended was his wallet, which was curiously alive, as if waiting for him to fetch it. It was a bulging black thing stuffed with cards and bits of paper, cash, a flat key that we didn't know what fit, a fingernail-size chip of mica, an old Saint Christopher medal engraved on the back with his mother's name. The wallet seemed wholly personal, the one thing that kept him alive. I tried putting it in the boxes we were packing, but every time I got it in a box, I had to take it out and put it back on the table. In the end, I carried the wallet with me on the ride home.

When we were done, the Bekins people were left in charge,

and Mother and I got back on the highway headed for Mississippi. She wanted to talk.

"It's not the movies, is it?" she said, looking out the car window. "Nothing changes. A point on your compass goes dark. In a few months it won't matter. It'll be like he never existed. That wallet is the only thing. He used it, needed it to carry out his life. Now he doesn't need it, but it's still ready to carry out a life. We'll put it in a nice drawer somewhere."

She'd cried a little when we left Houston, and on the empty highway outside of Lafayette. As we approached the Atchafalaya bridge, the twenty-mile bridge over the swamp, I caught her paying more attention than usual to the watery landscape, and I knew that she was feeling my father's absence. She rubbed at her cheeks, pinched the bridge of her nose, dabbed at the corners of her eyes as we clicked over the expansion joints on that endless bridge. In a while I stopped looking. I watched the road and felt my back ache, something across the shoulders, something I hadn't noticed before.

We made a couple of stops at gas stations and one at a place called Rollo-Burger and did most of the drive in silence until she found a Girl Groups compilation tape at an Exxon station outside of Baton Rouge. She played that the rest of the way home. It was chilly and gray, not quite wintry outside, but brisk enough to make the car windows cold to the touch. She was fond of the Shirelles, the Ronettes, the Chantels.

We unloaded a few boxes at Mother's house, ones she wanted to keep with her. I noticed that the horse was still tied to the tree down the street, and that the kite was still caught on the telephone wire behind the Terlinks'. She offered coffee, but it was late afternoon and I was anxious to get home.

"You want to come for dinner?" I said.

"No. I'll be fine."

"Maybe you'd better come."

"Why don't you call me later?" she said. "Maybe I'll come later."

I knew she wouldn't, but I smiled and gave her a hug, then got back in my car and headed along the coast toward Biloxi.

When I got to the house, RV was in her room eating a burrito, doing her homework, watching MTV, and talking on the telephone. She waved the burrito at me as I went by her door. I waved back, put my bag in the bedroom, then went into the kitchen where Jewel was cooking.

"How's your mother?" she said.

"She's been better," I said.

"You?"

"Same," I said. I went to the sink and washed my hands. "It's depressing stuff."

"I imagine it is," Jewel said. She put an arm around me and laid her head on my back. "It'll improve."

"I need some dark glasses," I said, looking out the kitchen window. "Everything looks bleak to me. Burned out. Like we've recently been bombed. Or we're recovering from being bombed ten years ago."

"That would be winter coming," Jewel said.

"Sometimes it's more desolate," I said.

"Take a Valium," she said.

"I tried that," I said. "Didn't work. Made things worse. It works if you're slightly depressed, but if you're really depressed, the depression gets worse." I went out onto the glassed-in back porch, sat in one of the chairs. Most of the light had slipped out of the sky, but I could still see the yard covered in leaves that were flipping over when they were caught by the breeze. Frank padded his way through the kitchen and stood beside my chair to get his head scratched. When he'd had enough, he hopped onto the sofa and propped his jaw on one foot.

"Maybe we should get another one of these," I said, over my shoulder.

"Another what?" Jewel said.

"Dog. Somebody for Frank to play with."

"Frank don't play," Jewel said.

"How old is he, anyway?"

"Early thirties." She brought a couple beers out to the porch, gave one to me, sat on the sofa with Frank, petting him.

A few minutes later RV came out and said, "Can I go to Mallory's for one minute?"

"One minute?" Jewel said.

"One," RV said. "Please?"

"If you're only going for one minute, it can't be that important," I said.

RV rolled her eyes and waved her hand at me dismissively.

"I guess," Jewel said. "Is she coming to get you?"

"Yeah. Unless you want to let me use the car," RV said, doing a Happy Meal grin.

"Perhaps not," Jewel said.

"So what have you done to advance the cause of the American teenager?" I said. "Been drinking a lot? Smoking a lot of weed? Other drugs? Having sex?"

"We rolled a house," RV said.

"I thought it was called wrapping," I said.

"Used to be, in the old days. Now it's rolling," she said.

"Things change much too fast," I said.

"It only seems that way because you're not out rolling houses," Jewel said.

"I wouldn't mind."

"It's kind of spooky," RV said. "We did this great house over on Shattles Street the other night." She turned to Jewel and said, "Well, can I go or what?"

"Fine, go. Be back by eight."

"Aw, Mom. Eight-thirty," RV said. "O.K.? Eight-thirty."

"Eight," Jewel said, flipping the back of her hand at her daughter, giving her the international scoot signal.

When RV was gone, after we had heard her footsteps trail all the way back to her room, I said, "So my father's dead and I guess that's the end of that. He's never going to be alive again."

"You've covered it there," Jewel said.

"This isn't the best I've ever felt," I said. "I'm just pawing at things, going through the steps, taking up space wherever I go. I don't feel awful or anything, I feel automatic."

"It gets better," she said.

RV came out of her room and went out the front door, slamming it behind her. "If she's only going for a minute, why did you say eight?"

"Saving her a call. We've still got the seven forty-five call to go. The extra thirty minutes."

I nodded. It surprised me how much went on between Jewel and RV that I barely caught. I pulled out my father's wallet, held it between my thumb and forefinger. "I've got his wallet."

"His wallet?" Jewel said.

"Yes." The wallet bulged in my hand like an enormous charcoal briquette.

"Put it away," Jewel said, giving *me* the scoot gesture. "We'll deal with it another time."

"Fine," I said. I slipped the wallet into my shirt pocket and took a long pull on my beer. "What now?"

"Dinner, TV, home life," Jewel said.

"What's dinner?"

"Lamb chops," she said. "The most wonderful lamb chops."

Jewel had found a storage place out off Hendrix Road, and we cleaned it up and took my mother out to have a look. On the following Monday, when the Bekins truck arrived, I had to supervise the unloading of my father's leftovers. The weather had turned balmy, but packing a condo's worth of possessions into the corrugated metal storage unit was sweaty work. All three of us were there, working alongside the three movers. We slid stuff down the long ramps attached to the back of the truck. I did a lot of organizing inside the shed. We had boxes of stuff piled up along one side, a few pieces of furniture stacked up high, and a few others out in the middle, so we could sit down. When the Bekins guys were gone, we rearranged things in the unit, then pulled down the corrugated door and padlocked it, and it seemed as though we were finally burying my father.

In the next week or so we spent some time toting up our losses and figuring how to get around them. Most of the money could sit on the credit cards, although when Jewel told me she'd seen a TV piece on credit-card debt and that the average debt was only four thousand dollars, that gave me pause, since we owed more than ten thousand, not all of it from gambling, spread across a half-dozen cards or more. Plus, we had the house, the cars, everything else to pay for.

"Our problem is we're small fry," I said to her one night when we were talking about gambling. "How can we win anything betting twenty-five dollars a hand? Everything is piecemeal for people like us, people our size."

The night before I'd watched a guy walk up to the craps table and get a ten-thousand-dollar marker by nodding at the pit boss. It was easy. The guy lost, got a second marker for the same amount, lost that. He got a third ten thousand and dropped that. The fourth time he got a marker the table turned around, and pretty soon this same guy had a hundred thousand dollars in front of him. He was dumping thousand-dollar chips on the hard ways. He paid his markers and still had sixty grand. He hit the hard eight three times in a row for nine thousand a shot. The dice were coming in. He was a loud guy, a big guy with cowboy written all over him. Everybody liked him. When he yelled, everybody yelled. He got all kinds of treatment — they let him hold three dice and throw two. He tossed the third back behind him, and one of the dealers had to scramble to jump on it.

"We have to beg to get any credit," I said. "Get the pit guy, the floor guy, tell a story, ask for something extra. Then the floor guy is solicitous but not sure he can help."

"You talking about that Phil person? He's nice."

"They're all nice," I said. "They go off and look at their slips of paper, then come back and say, 'Maybe I can go eight hundred, how's that?'"

"I don't know why you think this is a problem," Jewel said.

"Because we can't play enough to win anything," I said.

The shift guy we knew best was Phil Post. He was a family guy, he had a wife, kids, one in college at Tulane, doing real well. That's what we usually talked about until we needed something on the credit line. Then it was business. Then it was "Let's go look at the credit records, O.K.?" and we had to follow him over to the cashier and stand there waiting for help. Sooner or later Phil would come up with a marker for seven hundred, or maybe nine, and that was it. So we were forced to split the new money and sit and play quarters, hoping to get some cards, to get a run, win a few hands and boost the ticket.

When everything else went to hell, we went back to the slots. That was because one night when we were walking out of the casino Jewel thought she'd give the twenty-five-dollar slots a chance. She did, and bang, won a bundle. So we started looking for the big slots to rescue us whenever we were in trouble. I played the tens, mostly. I sat there transfixed by their peculiar beauty, the noise, the garishness, the roll of the spots past the windows, the payline, the extraordinary feeling I got each time the wheels came to a stop, one after another, left to right, click, click, click. The excitement stuffed into fractions of seconds between the first reel stopping and the second, between the second and the third. When I got a double diamond on the payline on the first reel, time seemed to slow way down while I waited for the second reel. And if that landed on something good, a double or triple bar, or a red seven, then I was instantly focused on the final window, and I waited, heat in the back of my neck. The whole process took maybe a full second, but it felt like an hour. I was surprised how fast I could snap focus from one reel to the next. Nine times out of ten the third reel came up unmatched and I got nothing, but once in a while it hit. So then I would play more, drop a few hundred dollars, later a few thousand. I'd lose nine hundred and win six. Or the reverse. Or I'd hit two thousand and put it back in, trying for more.

Once, when I was ahead maybe five thousand, Jewel tried to get me to leave. I said, "Yeah, just a minute."

"Let's go. We're up. It's a big win."

"Hang on," I said.

I went back to the ten machine and put the hundred-dollar bills in one at a time until I was down to twelve hundred dollars, maybe three hundred ahead for the night, and then Jewel said, "Well, it doesn't fucking matter now. Stuff it in there. Here, give me some." And she grabbed a few of the hundreds still in my hand.

I sometimes spent eighteen hours straight at the Paradise, so I knew the different player profiles — the cheerful tourists looking fresh and ruddy, with their wet-combed hair and bright polo shirts at eight in the morning; the out-of-work crowd at four in the afternoon; the party people at midnight; and the diehards at four A.M. I developed a gallery of weird faces, body language, physical expressions. I listened to too much gamblers' small talk — some drunk at the blackjack table saying he hadn't had sex in so long he didn't know which arm it was under. That was a big hit at midnight.

I played mostly swing and graveyard shifts, and I liked the people who played and the people who worked overnight. There was a lot of blear on the late shift, and there wasn't a lot of hope on people's faces. Nobody believed he or she was about to take down the big score. They were afraid to hope. They'd been there, they knew what was coming. They went grim and straight at it.

Earlier in the evening you got husband-and-wife teams, people who'd never gambled before. At ten o'clock you could play blackjack and there was a lot of laughter, a lot of fun. People were talking to each other, wising off, putting the rush on the dealer, making jokes when they lost bets. By four in the morning there weren't many jokes left, and the ones that remained were meaner. You could feel the dealer feeling bad for the big loser, and each dealer had a way of expressing it. Some guys would slap cards on the table as if the extra velocity would turn the spots in the player's favor. Some were deadly quiet while they drew five cards to twenty-one. Some swept losing bets away fast, as if that might minimize the pain.

"Maybe we're born to lose," Jewel said one night when we'd decided not to go to the Paradise. "Natural born losers."

"This is not a good attitude," I said. "Why would that be? What happened to morphic resonance?"

"We haven't done all that well, Ray," she said.

"That doesn't mean we'll always lose. What about Voodoo

Takes Over? Or the hypothesis of the cumulative memory of nature? Any minute you could be a big winner."

"I guess," she said.

After all our calculating was done, the ATM slips sorted, the checkbook balanced, the credit-card statements consulted, to that moment we were out a couple thousand more than we thought.

Thursday before Thanksgiving we were settling in to watch *ER* when I told Jewel I was feeling kind of lucky and was thinking of stepping over to the Paradise. She shook her head and said, "Dangerous feeling."

"You want to go? We can tape this. Go for a while. We haven't been much since Houston."

"We haven't lost any money since Houston either," Jewel said.

"You better stay home, Bob," RV said from the next room. "I think that's what Mom's trying to tell you."

"Thanks, doll," I said over my shoulder. "I needed a clarification."

"You need something," Jewel said.

"Hey, don't worry. It's all right. I'll play a few hands and if nothing magic happens I'll come home. I'll be back by midnight. You want to go?"

"Not me. Not tonight." She waved a hand. "Go. Go."

I felt guilty leaving the house, but then I was out and driving, and it was great to be alive — I felt free and young, the way I used to feel when I was eighteen, going on a date in my father's car. I stopped at a gas station, used one of the credit-card pumps, and watched the scattered rain pop the concrete. I got out on 90 and drove fast, the radio thumping. It was chilly out, colder than usual, and I had the heater on. I liked the way it smelled, liked the way it sounded. The windshield wipers clacked as I drove toward Gulfport, then made a U-turn on the highway, short of the Edgewater Mall, and drove back to the Paradise. I steered into the garage and pulled into a space on the first floor.

By the look of things, the number of cars, the place wasn't too crowded. I walked through the hollow-sounding garage and across the concrete bridge to the casino, rain tapping on the canvas awning over the entrance. Outside, I couldn't hear the slot machines at all, but as soon as I opened the door they were there in 3D Surround Sound. By the escalator there was a poster of a craps table with the headline "Winners Know When to Quit," slugged with a telephone number for Gamblers Anonymous. I stopped at the bar and got a beer, then walked past the craps tables and the roulette tables to the blackjack pits. I shook hands and watched the play at one table after another. Dealers and pit people asked where I'd been and I said I'd been practicing.

A dealer named Ed Romeo pointed to third base at his five-dollar table and nodded at me. "Take a seat," he said.

"Cards O.K.?" I said.

"I've seen worse," Ed Romeo said.

"I need to get a marker," I said.

Ed Romeo called over his shoulder to ask the pit person, a wiry woman in her forties who wore thick glasses and had mop-like red hair, if I could get a marker. She smiled, put an arm on my shoulder, kissed me on the cheek. "We can do whatever Raymond wants," she said, patting me.

"A thousand," I said. "I'll start with that."

She had a name tag with "Rebecca" on it in quarter-inch letters, and under that, where everyone else had "Trenton," or "Atlantic City," or "Reno," she had "Sunnybrook."

"Let's hope it's your only thousand for the night," she said. "Maybe you can turn it into five."

"Why stop there?" I said.

She went to the island behind the dealers and got on the phone, then went into a drawer and got some plastic buttons, two, each with "500" written on it. She brought the buttons out, put them on the side of the dealer's chip rack. "Give him a thousand," she told Ed Romeo. He pulled out five blacks and a tall stack of green chips.

"Half in green?" he said.

"Better give me some red," I said. "I'm starting slow."

"Sure," he said. He counted four hundred in green, pulled out some reds, counted a hundred in red, then lined up the black, green, and red stacks in front of him. "A thousand out," he said over his shoulder.

Rebecca looked up from where she was standing over the computer terminal. "Send it," she said.

He slid the chips across the tabletop to me, and I pulled the stacks back and to my left, then dropped ten dollars out on the spot in front of me. Ed Romeo had been changing decks when I arrived. Now he held the two decks out with a yellow card on top, pointed the cards at the player to my right, a crabby-faced Asian woman, quite short. She cut the cards. The guy on the other side of the table was playing two spots, a quarter each. There was a woman playing nickels next to him, then the Asian woman, then me.

"So what's been up?" I said.

"My wife got on as a dealer," Ed Romeo said. "She's working down here. It's her first night."

"You told me she was in school," I said.

"Yeah. She aced it. They wanted her out fast so they're starting her on single deck," he said.

The cards came and went. I raised my bet to a quarter and then was betting two spots. Money came, then went away, then came back. There wasn't any pattern to the way things were going.

Ed Romeo said, "I haven't seen you in a while. You been playing someplace else?"

"Out of town," I said. "My father died."

He made a face. "I'm sorry to hear that."

"Happens to everybody, doesn't it?"

"Sure does," he said. "Is Jewel with you?"

"She's at home watching *ER*," I said. "What time is it, anyway?"

He flipped his hands twice for the cameras, then looked at his watch. "Closing in on ten," he said.

Rebecca came back and stood at the edge of the table, putting her hand on my shoulder, watching me play. "How're we doing?"

"Same as ever," I said, showing her my cards.

"Oh, Mr. Thirteen," she said. "This doesn't look too promising. Maybe you ought to try Tanya over on two-oh-four. Her rack's low. I don't know if it's people buying and leaving, or if she's paying, but it's something."

I slid out two fifty-dollar bets. I'd lost a few hundred and change at the table and was getting ready to leave. When the cards came, I got a blackjack on one and a stiff on the other, hit the stiff and busted. I waited until the cards were played out for all the other players and shoved my chips back across the line toward Ed Romeo. "Color these, will you?" I said.

"Color coming in," the dealer said.

"Go," Rebecca said.

Ed Romeo matched up some new chips — a five hundred, a

hundred, and three greens — alongside the chips I had given him. "Look right?" he said to Rebecca.

"Fine," she said, waving her pen toward me.

He pushed the chips across. Rebecca wrote something on the paper she had, which she had pulled out from behind the shuffle machine, then tucked the paper into her clipboard.

"You're going to Tanya?" she said.

"I thought I'd give her a try." I nodded at Ed Romeo and climbed off the stool.

I stopped to talk to another dealer I sometimes played with, a guy named Strobe, who was standing at the edge of the High Stakes Salon. He was red-faced and in his late thirties. His wife worked at the casino as a cocktail waitress and, according to him, made more than he did as a dealer. We were talking about Strobe's boat when a guy who looked like David Duke walked by with a young girl who had follow-the-bouncing-ball breasts.

"Is that him?" I said.

"Yep. Comes over all the time," Strobe said. He smoothed the front of his tux shirt. "Sometimes I wonder why somebody doesn't just pop him. He's a smug little son of a bitch."

"Not little," I said. "Looks like he's six two."

"He's little in the head," Strobe said. "Has that frail thing."

"Who's his friend?" I said.

"Never saw her before. She's got volatility there in the front, doesn't she?"

Tanya, the dealer I was going to play with, was a tall, thin blond woman in her late twenties. She walked by and rubbed the back of my arm. "Hi, sweetie," she said.

She had dark green metallic fingernails. I grabbed her hand for a closer look. "These are terrific," I said.

"Thanks. You're the only one who thinks so. Everybody else says they look slutty."

"Well?" I said.

"Yeah, that's what I say," Tanya said.

"I was coming to play with you. You're on break?"

"Coming back from break," she said. "Cards are pretty good tonight."

"Great. I'll be there in a minute. You can dump the rack. Hold third base, will you?"

"Sure thing," Tanya said.

Three Vietnamese women were talking loud and fast in Vietnamese at a table in front of us. "Look at this, will you?" Strobe said, twisting his neck as if he were trying to crack it. "I shouldn't say anything, never mind. I got no idea what they think they're doing. They win sometimes, but Jesus God, the way they play."

"I thought they were usually pretty good," I said.

"Some are," he said. "Not these three." He ran a finger around the inside of the collar of his tux shirt, adjusted his bow tie.

I patted his shoulder. "I'm going over here and steal some money from Tanya."

"Stay away from me," he said, jerking a thumb over his shoulder toward the salon. "I'm burning. Don't even come close."

"You're always burning."

"It's worse tonight. And it's not changing. Save yourself. Stay away."

We shook hands and I started around the cluster of blackjack tables toward 204.

The shift manager, Phil Post, was coming toward the blackjack pit from the main cashier's cage. He stopped. "How're things?" he said.

"Don't know yet," I said. "Got any advice?"

"Go home?" Phil said.

"Who you got dealing there?" I said.

Phil Post was always pleasant, always commiserating, urging us to leave when we were ahead or when we got even after a bad run of cards. He seemed genuinely friendly, but he worked for the Paradise, so who knew. He was paid to grease the skids, to shill, so it didn't matter whether he was friendly or not, because even if he was, even if everything he said to us and everybody else he dealt with was as genuine as the day was long, it still amounted to coaxing more money out of our pockets.

"Nobody's dealing there, that's the point," he said. "I'm trying to save you some money."

"I might win, though," I said.

"I might date Marilyn Monroe in the afterlife," Phil said. "But I'm not making book on it."

I caught the eye of a dealer named Hazel who I'd played with a number of times. I waved, she waved.

"Look," Phil said. "If the cards don't come, get up and leave. That's my advice."

"Will do," I said.

Phil rattled the papers he had in his hand. His eyes were watery, like he was stoned. "Got to take care of the guests," he said. "See you later?"

I played with Tanya until ten-thirty, playing fast, losing the thousand then winning half of it back. The cards were good, but my betting was erratic. I got hung out on a couple of big bets. Then I caught cards on a couple of small ones. I was five hundred down and that didn't seem too bad. I thought about going home, but decided to wait. I got a comp from Rebecca and went upstairs for a hamburger at the restaurant. I sat by a window overlooking the lighted piers in the shrimpers' marina behind the Paradise. There were people working out there, going back and forth, on and off the boats, making big gestures, tugging around on the nets. They were all bundled against the rain that slashed across the sky.

Shortly after eleven I was back at Ed Romeo's table, only Ed Romeo had taken off early, so I was playing with Tildra, a short, black-haired woman who told a lot of dirty jokes and more than most wanted her players to win. Like all dealers, she gave advice, but hers was book perfect. She'd been dealing for ten years, and she played at other casinos when she wasn't working. I went to hit fours against a five and she shook her head, refused to give me a card.

"What?" I said.

She pointed at the fours, wagging her forefinger.

"Split?"

"Against five and six," she said.

I put out another twenty-five-dollar chip to match my original bet. As it turned out, I lost both.

I won for the first hour. I was a thousand dollars ahead, then fifteen hundred. I was increasing my bets and winning. The cards were coming. Tildra and her relief were pleased for me. I tipped heavily when I was winning. If I bet a hundred, I tipped a quarter. The way the tips worked, if I won, the dealer won double what I bet for her. By midnight I was up two thousand dollars.

Tildra said, "Now you ought to go home."

"You think?" I said.

She rolled her eyes. "What do I have to do, come over there and slap you silly?"

"No, hey, I can take a hint," I said. I colored up and took my purple chips to the cashier's cage and got my money. Since they didn't have anything larger than hundred-dollar bills, the three thousand made a fair-size wad that I couldn't easily get into my wallet. I put the money in my pants pocket, walked the length of the casino, and stood outside in the breezeway.

I was anxious to tell Jewel. I thought about calling her, then thought I'd better wait. It was rainy and pretty out there, and I was overwhelmed with my good fortune, and thought how much I loved Jewel and RV. Asian music came across the water from the fishing boats where the people worked. Shaded bulbs were strung from ropes that clanked against the masts. Water was cracking over rocks that ran alongside the jetty behind the casino hotel. Occasionally some fish disturbed the water and the surface opened and there was a splash.

The rain had slowed and there was fog gathering, though I could see high clouds moving fast. I watched them slide and wished Jewel was there to see. I was feeling lucky to have her, RV, the house, Frank — everything. I was in love with all of it. I pictured them in bed, asleep, Frank with RV. I had a perfect TV image of them. The bedroom just light enough to see their contented faces against the pillows. I stuck my hand down in my pocket and felt the thickness of the bills, and a chill caught my neck. I thought I'd get RV a Vespa of her own, an old one, silver, maybe blue, the kind that always showed up in French movies. I put my hands on the round steel railing, felt the cold wet metal, looked over the side at the debris floating in the water. There was a Styrofoam take-out box, there were cups, there was a plastic bottle. Midnight was a wonderful time. When the rain picked up I stepped back so that I was under the second-floor balcony between the casino and the hotel. The concrete in front of me was white with rain, reflecting the floodlights that shined on it. I dried my hands on my pants, listening to the water rush down the sides of the building. The pink and lime neon of the casino decoration was reflected in the rain. Upstairs, there were silhouettes of people inside, behind glass doors, looking out. Behind them, other people played slots.

I thought about what I was going to do next. I knew I should take the two thousand I was ahead and come another night, try to win another two. That way, over time, I might win back what we'd lost. But I felt good and I knew I wasn't leaving. I was going to play. It was my casino, my night. If I didn't hit it at the tail end of swing, I'd get it on graveyard at three. That was my shift, anyway. The dealers were all friends, my people, and I would win, as if by magic. This time, this night. This was my moment. I had three thousand dollars. That was a stake. I was going to move to the salon, where there were twenty-five- and fifty-dollar tables, hundred-dollar tables if you wanted them, where the felt was blue and there were only five spots per table instead of seven.

Rain spattered the concrete, the steel railing, the otherwise serene water of the Mississippi Sound — a sweet static, hushed and reverent. Full of potential. I thought again of calling Jewel and telling her what I was going to do, but I knew that might break the spell. She might talk some sense into me, and the one thing I didn't want was sense. The one thing I didn't need, could not use, the one thing that would not help me, was sense.

The tall lights of the marina reflected in the water, shimmering, rippled strips that faded to nothing. There were half a dozen scrawny trees in large wooden planters on the walkway getting their fill of rain. I don't know how I knew this was my night, I just did. Risk everything. No losing.

A boat pulled out of the marina, its two bright searchlights swiveling past me as it turned to go out into the sound. Caught in the light, the rain looked as if it were hopping on the walk. I thought back over the past few months, the other times I'd played at the casino, the people I'd met, the winners, the losers. I remembered going to the men's room once and, while I was drying my hands, seeing a guy walk in counting a fistful of hundreds. The guy went into a toilet stall and went on counting. I could see his feet as he stood there and went through his stack of hundred-dollar bills. The bills made this flip flip flip sound as he counted.

I'd played enough at the casino to know that if I was going to win, I was going to have to push my luck. I wasn't going to outplay them, or outthink them, and I wasn't going to outwait them — they had too much money for that. If I was going to get them, I was going to get them by surprise. By the grace of God, good luck, and surprise. Nothing else. For some reason I *knew* it would work. I was certain. I was as sure of that as I was of anything in the world. All I had to do was go inside, pay attention, play crazy, and win very big.

It was an impulse I'd felt before, but never paid attention to. I usually got scared when the bets went up. At two hundred I was shaky, at five I was frying. Money moved fast when you played five hundred a hand. I'd gotten myself up six thousand one night, playing that way, before losing it. And when money moved fast, it could move either way. The key was picking the moment to bail. I hadn't done well with that, but there was always a first time.

The rain dropped off again and the surface of the sound went glazed, the lights suddenly focused, reflected, diving down into the water. I looked out at the foot of the marina and saw only tall columns of yellow and white light. It was my turn, my time. I laughed, scrubbed a palm over my forehead, and went inside.

I heard nothing. The rattling gibberish of the machines, the jackpots bonging off, the twirling reels and people shouting craps calls, the piped-in music, the change machines counting coins, the jabbering of the patrons — none of it registered. I went to the main cashier, took out a MasterCard, put it on the counter. "See if you can get me five thousand on this."

The cashier was a woman named Kathleen, with whom I usually joked about the small increments of my withdrawals. She looked at me and at the card as if we were both strangers. "Are you sure about this, Ray?" she said.

"Yep," I said. "And there's more where that came from. That card is blemish free."

The cashier area was like a bank, five or six teller windows and a couple of other areas with computers. Kathleen went to one of the computers, slipped my card through the reader, typed in my Paradise ID number. I watched her. She was a pleasant-looking woman in her forties — someone who would look out of place in the casino without the outfit.

In a minute she looked up from the computer and said, "Won't do it."

"What do you mean?"

"Won't give you five thousand. Says I have to call them," she said.

"Fine," I said. "While you're at it, try this one, too." I reached into my back pocket for my wallet, pulled out a second credit card, flipped that out onto the counter. "Five on this one as well, please."

"What are you going to do, break the bank?" She picked up the second card, fed it through the card reader, then got the phone to call Customer Service on the first card.

"They're just checking to make sure it's me," I said.

That's what it was. The Customer Service people had to speak to me, get some identification from me, get my mother's maiden name, and then they O.K.'d the deal. The second card didn't bother to ask. When Kathleen brought the two five-thousand-dollar checks for me to sign, she said, "You know, we can pick up the charges on these."

The charges amounted to more than three hundred dollars each, so I thanked her and said, "Please."

"I'll call shift," she said. "He's got to sign it." She took the two checks into the back, returned a minute later with signatures and two other sheets of paper for me to sign. I signed them, and she counted out ten thousand dollars. I tried to get her to leave the cash in its wraps, but she wouldn't do that. She had to count it, and she had to have two people stand there and verify the exchange. When she finally released the money to me, I stacked it up and folded it over, pulled the three thousand out of my pocket and wrapped it around the ten, then thanked Kathleen.

That's when Phil Post showed up. "What are you going to do with all this?" he said, signing the receipts for the casino to pay the freight for the cash advances.

"Play some blackjack. Do a little dance," I said.

"I don't know," he said. "You sure this is a good idea?"

"It's my night, Phil," I said. "I feel it. I'm already up. I'm going up more. All that money you guys have taken from me over the last couple of months? Coming home tonight."

"God, I hope so," he said. "Nothing would please me more than to see the nice guys like you and Jewel end up big winners. Where is she, anyway?"

"She's not playing tonight," I said. "She's resting on her laurels."

"She know you're playing this big?"

"She knows. She knows," I said.

Post laughed and clapped me on the shoulder. "Listen. If it starts going bad, you get out. You hear me? I don't want to see you coming back for more."

"Never happen," I said. "I'm only getting this so the stuff I take from you will have some company."

Phil Post laughed.

"Dream a little dream," I said, laughing at myself and trying to make sure that he knew that's what I was doing.

"You're in the salon?" Phil said.

"Yep," I said. "Going down there now. What time is it?"

"Twelve-thirty, twelve forty-five, something like that." He tapped the watch on his wrist. "This sucker isn't working the way it once did."

I had a table all to myself with a woman named Bambi dealing. That's what her name tag said, "Bambi." When I finally asked, she said it was real.

"Bambi what?" I said.

"Locks," she said. "Bambi Locks."

She was dealing a six-deck shoe. I got ten thousand dollars' worth of chips — five oranges, four grand in five-hundred-dollar chips, one in blacks, and started playing two hands at two hundred a hand. I went through my blacks right away, cashed another thousand for blacks, and started to go through that when I hit a run of cards. I got that thousand back, and the first thousand, and a thousand more. I was going two hands at five hundred now, and Bambi was dealing fast.

I moved to three hands at five and was hitting pretty good, winning two out of three, sometimes all three, doubling down and splitting when I had the cards. When I was up four thousand dollars, I bumped my bet to a thousand but played only two spots. The big orange chip looked small out on the betting circle compared to the stacks of blacks I'd been playing. I split a couple of hands like that, then jacked the bets up to two thousand on each of two spots. Bambi called out, "Orange in action," and dealt the cards. I dropped both of those bets and another pair like them. Then I pushed one and won one for three thousand. A quick check of the chips in front of me said I was down a grand.

"We have to do this?" I said, pointing at the table-limit card, which said that the maximum bet was three thousand.

"They'll raise it," Bambi said.

"Get them to make it five, will you?" I said.

She called the pit guy, spoke to him over her shoulder, and he nodded. "Fine," he said. He wrote something down on a pad.

I bet five thousand dollars on each of two spots, having to make up the second five with bills from my pocket. I got twenty on each hand and in my excitement kicked over my chair trying to slide out of it and stand at the table, waiting for Bambi to roll her down card. She'd dealt herself a nine up. I waved across the tops of both of my betting spots. When she flipped a queen I shouted and banged the foam-filled cushion around the edge of the table. The pit guy came out to get the chair as Bambi measured off my ten thousand.

"Great hit," she said.

"Thanks," I said. I pulled the money back away from the spots and grabbed my shoulders right at the neck, trying to loosen the knots. "Now what?" I said.

I put two thousand on each spot and the cards came out. Two more winners. Again, and again winners, and I spread my bets to three spots at a thousand. I lost a couple, won a double, lost a split. The hands were going by fast, the cards were pouring out of the shoe, and my betting and drawing off winnings, and Bambi's dealing and paying and sweeping lost bets synchronized like a perpetual-motion machine. We played this way for ten minutes or more — I wasn't tracking the time or how much I was ahead. I had ten-high stacks of five-hundred-dollar chips, lopsided stacks, some taller than others, four tall stacks of hundreds, and a single stack of the orange thousands. The cards were running so sweetly that I nursed my bets on the three spots back up to five thousand, then seven, after I got another increase in the table limit. I looked at my chips and knew that I could never lose them, there were too many stacks, the cards were too good. I bumped my three bets to ten thousand, scarcely believing it myself, and at the same time not at all nervous, not wary, just certain of the cards to come. And they did — two pair of faces, and a nineteen against a jack of spades that Bambi had up. I waved her off and she smiled happily, as if she knew I had her beaten. Casually she flipped her down card with the corner of the jack. Was an ace.

I felt that. An electric shock, a two-by-four brought down across my back. Thirty thousand dollars swept away. She didn't look up. Something forced me to bet five thousand on each of the three spots without pausing, and I got three stiff hands that I had to hit against a face card, and lost all three. That's when I stopped to count what was in front of me. Fifteen thousand three hundred.

"Can't win if you don't play," I said, sliding that out in three stacks. Five thousand on each spot with a hundred tip riding. That was it. No more chips. The cards came. Bambi's up card was an ace of diamonds. I quickly flipped my hands. I had seventeen, thirteen, and a pair of tens. She tucked her second card and asked if I wanted insurance. I was shocked. I held out both hands and said, "Wait a minute, please."

She stood across from me with one hand on the shoe and the other at her chest. "I'm not going anywhere," she said. "You take your time."

I stepped back from the table and ran my hands through my hair. Insurance was a sucker bet unless you were counting. I tried to call up some memory of how many of the ten-value cards were out. I looked to see where we were in the shoe. I'd have to get more money to insure the hands. The twenty might be worth insuring, the thirteen surely wasn't. I rubbed my eyes and rocked back from the table, sighed, finally cut my hand across the top of my betting spots to turn down the insurance. "No," I said. "I can't, no."

Bambi still didn't move. "You're sure?"

"Yes," I said, taking another deep breath, blowing it out in almost a whistle.

She leaned forward and slowly eased the corner of her cards into the peeper, built into the tabletop so dealers with aces up could check for blackjacks without lifting their down cards. Her shoulders sank and at the same time I saw her head begin to shake. She pushed the cards forward, turned over a bright-colored king.

I felt as if rows of needles were running along the tops of my shoulders and up both sides of my neck into the scalp behind my ears. Bambi pulled my three bets and the tips, and said, "Thanks for the try." Then she collected the cards.

I stood there watching her straighten the table. I'd been

playing maybe twenty-five minutes. My ears were ringing. I couldn't quite figure out how much I'd bet, where I was. To lose thirty, fifteen, fifteen, I had to have been ahead fifty, plus the ten I started with.

"I bet thirty, then fifteen twice, right?"

"Yes," Bambi said.

Up fifty thousand dollars. The needles were spreading across my upper back. Phil Post came up with seven hundred that was the payback on the credit-card charges.

"What happened?" He clawed my shoulder.

"Don't know. I was great, I was killing you. Then — things turned."

Phil counted the seven hundred into my hand. "Maybe this will help a little. You got some of the ten left?"

"Sure, I got plenty," I said, folding one of the hundreds and handing it back to Post, who waved it off.

"Take me to dinner some night," he said.

"O.K.," I said.

I felt like a robot. I pulled the cash out of my pocket. I had two thousand. I gave it to Bambi, along with the money Post brought, and asked for black chips. I played one spot for a hundred. I did that for a while, playing automatically, not paying attention, winning and losing some, the cards going back and forth. My head was ringing. I wasn't really there. I was trying to get a grip. After a while I jumped my bet to two hundred, and then, when the cards weren't coming, I backed down to one.

A couple of college kids came up and started playing quarters. They were drinking and screwing around with a hundred dollars' worth of five-dollar chips. It was a quarter table, so they were betting piles of five, and the way the cards were running, they won as much as they lost, so their hundred kept them in.

When Bambi hit the cut card and started shuffling the

six decks, the two kids headed off for the bathroom, and the pit guy, whose name was Scooter and who looked like casino scum right out of the movies, slid around to my side of the table and said, "Want a hundred-dollar table?"

I shook my head. "No. They're fine with me. They don't bother me."

"I can do it if you want to," Scooter said. "They got no business over here anyway."

"None of us has any business over here, Scooter."

"You got that right," he said.

"Shuffle through," Bambi said, packing the cards back against the shoe, flipping the yellow cut card to me.

"Could we make this my special shoe?" I said to her as I cut the cards.

"I'm trying," Bambi said.

I slid five blacks into my circle and she dealt. I won a couple of quick hands, then lost one on which I'd split sixes and had to split a second time, dropping fifteen hundred on that hand. I only had about three hundred left in front of me. "Hold these, will you?" I said, pointing to my playing spots. "I'm going to the cage."

I got another five thousand dollars from Kathleen and played on that until two-thirty. Then I was busted.

I wouldn't let myself think of quitting, but things had moved much faster than I'd anticipated. I was in worse shape now than ever, liquidation country. Still I was excited, filled with a sense of abandon that I hadn't felt in so long that I couldn't remember when I *had* felt it.

Money had shot across the table. I was up, down, then up further ahead than I'd ever been, or thought of being, but I didn't notice, and dumped it all. I was down sixteen thousand for the night and wandering around the casino, figuring my next move. Down like that, another five thousand didn't make any difference. I had to try.

I went to the washroom upstairs, rinsed my hands, patted water on my face, dried off with a paper towel out of the dispenser. Some guy standing at a urinal was talking to his buddy about having lost three hundred dollars. The guy was really mad. I heard it in his voice, his anger echoing in the men's room. I swiped at the shoulders and lapels of my jacket, wondering why I wasn't mad.

As I went down the escalator and walked to the cashier, I thought about my father, about how he was a better gambler than I was. Of course, he would never have played for five hundred dollars a hand, let alone what I was doing. Money was still money to him. Tonight, for me, was a chance to play. The way I played was a kind of probable suicide, but there was always that one chance I'd catch a streak just right, get in and get out. I knew I was way out of my league, playing the way I was. Lots of people could afford it, I just wasn't one of them. But it didn't bother me that much, and I was surprised that it didn't, that I wasn't nervous when I'd been betting large every hand. I'd calmed down since the real big bets, and playing seemed comfortable, felt right. It was a joy to see the money move at a sedate pace back and forth across the table, as if it had a life of its own, or was reacting to my will, or the dealer's, or even the magic in the cards. It was thrilling to see stacks of blacks coming at me, to see purples in play, to watch my hands and the cards, and to be at the table when the cards turned perfect for a few hands, so that when I hit a sixteen I *knew* my next would be a four or five, when I doubled my elevens I was sure of getting the face.

I gave Kathleen another credit card and asked for five thousand. I had a walletful of cards. Two that were over limit now, the one Jewel had finished and the one I'd finished off tonight, one that was half done, two others that had two or three thousand apiece on them, with limits of ten.

I said to Kathleen, "I wonder if you can set me up with a line of credit, in case I have to write a check."

"I can do the paperwork tonight, but I can't set up the line. Takes twenty-four hours," she said.

I gave her a fatigued look. "C'mon," I said. "I've lost a bunch. Maybe you could do me a favor?"

"I wish I could. Really. Let me call the shift manager for you."

"Phil?" I said.

"Yes," she said. "He'll have to do it."

"O.K.," I said.

When Phil Post came, he said the same thing that Kathleen said, but then he sort of shrugged and said, "Well, maybe we can work something. How much do you want?"

"I don't know," I said. "Ten, maybe fifteen thousand."

He smiled a weak, sort of sad smile. "You don't want to do that, Ray. We're not going to be able to, anyway. I can tell you that. Let me look into it and see what I can do."

I put my hand on his shoulder. "Just so we're clear, Phil," I said. "I do want to do it, O.K.? If you can. Thanks."

"Don't thank me," Phil said. "My advice was go home. It's still go home." He said it in a way that made me both like him and despise him. It was the gentlest sentiment that could have been offered, and at the same time it was wholly ignorant of the condition I was in, it ignored everything — the losses, the excitement, the hope, the desperation, the high. All of it. It was nonsense, a Hallmark card.

I smiled at Phil Post.

We had to do the telephone business with the Customer Service people at another one of the card companies, but I finally got my money and left the receipt for Post to sign for the cashier. I went back down to the blackjack salon.

For a while I stood behind a Vietnamese guy who had two ten-thousand-dollar racks of hundred-dollar chips. The guy had a hundred-dollar table all to himself. He was playing three spots. I nodded at the dealer, a woman named Margie.

She said, "Hey, Ray. How you doing?"

"Hitting 'em hard," I said.

She smiled at that and kept on dealing, machine-like, to the Asian guy. I skirted the next table, said hello to Sharon, a dealer I never played with because she always beat me. She smiled. There were two pit people, Claire and Coyle, working four tables open in the salon. I nodded at both of them as I took a seat with a favorite dealer, Lisette, who was dealing a two-deck pitch game. It was already a fifty-dollar table, and there was a heavyset gray-haired guy playing the last two spots. I dropped the five thousand in front of me and waited for Lisette to finish the deck. The guy was getting good cards, playing two spots at two hundred to five hundred each. He had what looked like seven or eight thousand in front of him.

After the shuffle, Lisette took my money and counted it out onto the tabletop, placing the bills in rows, one on top of the other, offset enough so that the camera in the ceiling could check her count.

"Purple and black?" she said.

"Right," I said. "You been O.K.?"

"Oh, sure," she said. "I've got trouble with my kid skipping school and getting caught, doing dope. You know, the usual." She finished stacking my chips, called them out and got them checked by the pit person, pushed them across to me. "I heard you were burning earlier."

"Yeah. It was amazing. I was up huge but it went out of control."

"Bambi told me. I'm sorry. Maybe we can turn it around,"

she said. "The cards are running." She introduced me to the guy playing third base. His name was Jack Delaplane.

I said hello when Lisette introduced us.

Delaplane said, "Why don't we play one and one? Two spots have been working."

"Fine by me," I said. "I'm looking for a slow start."

"How long have you been here?" Lisette said.

"Since about nine," I said. I put two black chips in my betting circle. Delaplane put out a five-hundred-dollar chip. The cards came.

A couple of hands later we forgot about the one and one, and each of us was playing two spots. Lisette dealt fast but funny, with the deck held back up at her chest and the cards shooting from there to our spots. The cards spun out, the way she dealt. Sometimes she counted my cards for me. She made jokes and chatted about how much she hated the drips who worked the pit. I'd caught her at the first of her shift, so we had forty minutes, and when she left to go on break, I had come back three thousand.

The relief dealer was a kid named Dave who I'd played with before, and when he took over the cards went cold. I got thirteens, fourteens, fifteens. In the twenty minutes Lisette was gone, I lost six thousand.

When she came back, I had a thousand dollars bet on each of two spots. She looked at this and did some kind of mock scream. "What are you doing? What happened to our chips?"

"Dave happened," I said.

"Why don't you get up and leave when he starts?" she said. "Mark and walk."

"Next time," I said. "I didn't plan to lose."

"Get those bets off there," she said, shooing them with her hand. "You're scaring the cards. Wait till I clean them up."

I withdrew my bets, leaving a hundred on each of the spots. The cards didn't change. I lost more, but I bet low until she shuffled. After that I had fifteen hundred dollars and bet three spots of five each. I lost two and won one, bet the thousand on one spot, and lost that. I shoved away from the table and asked Lisette to hold my place. She slid clear markers out onto the first two spots.

I was feeling crazy. I went back to Kathleen at the cashier's desk, pulled out the credit cards I thought I had money on, flipped them onto the granite countertop. "Start at five thousand on each of these, will you? Go down by five hundred until they give you something," I said.

"Are you sure about this?" she said. Kathleen seemed concerned for me.

"Yes, Kathleen. Thanks," I said.

She went to the computer and swiped the first card through. I reached into my pants pocket and pulled out a couple of hundreds I found there. The craps tables were close, so I went over there and put the two hundred down and asked for chips. "What're the dice doing?" I said to the stick man.

"They be sleepy," he said.

I put fifty dollars on the Don't Come. A cowboy at the other end of the table was in mid-roll. The point was four. His first roll after my bet was a seven.

"Bad timing," said the stick man.

"Now you tell me," I said. I put down fifty on the pass line and the guy came out with an eight. I put my last hundred behind in odds, and the guy threw seven.

The box man looked up at me and shrugged, as if to apologize. I smiled at him and shook my head. "It goes that way," I said.

"Sometimes," he said.

The guy working the stick said, "Cold wind. Sorry."

I patted his shoulder. "Don't worry."

I went back to the cashier. Kathleen said, "I got eight off of two cards. I didn't try the third one."

"Which is the third one?" When she waggled a gold Visa at me, I said, "Give me that. I'll keep that in reserve."

She finished the paperwork and signing and counted out the eight thousand.

"Oh, yeah," she said. "Phil Post said you could have two thousand as your line of credit, if you want it."

"I want it," I said.

"You want a marker or you want to write me a check?"

"I'll write you a check."

Lisette dealt good cards right off the bat, and soon I was betting a thousand dollars a hand, so I went up fast. Between four and four-forty, I ran the ten thousand to sixteen and change. Then I stayed out for Dave's relief and came back just after five.

The cards felt funny, stiff and plastic. I said, "What's this? New cards?"

"Yep. They made me do it," Lisette said, tossing her hair back. "I begged, but no good."

In the next forty minutes I lost the sixteen thousand I had on the table and another four I got from Kathleen off the last Visa card, putting me thirty-five and change down for the night. I'd tried to push it when I was winning, tried to get it back up to where it had been earlier. My largest bet was an eight-inch stack of hundred-dollar chips, four thousand, and I watched it walk. Lisette was doing everything she could to help me. Several times she ditched the deck because the cards were coming out bad. Once she went through a special shuffle she said ought to turn the cards around. She almost never let me take insurance, closing it fast so I wouldn't waver and take it when it was a bad bet. Still, I lost everything I looked at. At twenty minutes to six, when she was getting ready to go on break, I was alone at her table with no chips and no way to get any. My ears were ringing again. The bright lights in the ceiling focused on the tabletop, warmed the backs of my hands. All the pit people were going wide of the table. They always got scarce if you were taking a beating.

Lisette said, "Sorry, Ray. Jesus. This really pisses me off. They were going so good for a while."

"It's O.K.," I said, then laughed at that, laughed at hearing myself say it was O.K. I put my head down on the table. "You're going on break now?"

"Yeah," she said. "Can I get you something? You going to play more?"

"I don't think I can," I said. "Not until nine, anyway. I can go to the bank at nine."

"Opens eight-thirty," she said. "What bank?"

"First American," I said.

"Eight-thirty," she said.

I was trying to remember how much money I had in the bank. I didn't have much. I had a money-market checking account, so I could get money from that. I had a few grand there, in the account we'd started for RV's college. Short of selling things, that was all I could get my hands on. There was Jewel's salary, some in IRA and Keogh accounts. But with the cards loaded, I was close to the end of my easy-access bankroll.

I walked with Lisette down past the cashier's cage, where she turned off toward the elevator that went up to the break room. I went through the casino, out the side door by the parking garage. The concrete walk led down to the piers and the fishing boats. I wasn't sure what I wanted to do, so I went into the garage, opened the Explorer, climbed in, sat down, locked it up. I looked at my watch. I bent my head forward and rested it on the steering wheel. I tried to remember how I'd gotten into all this, how I'd gotten so far behind. I could see specific hands — the ten-thousand win, the big-bet losses, dealers drawing out on me, dramatic bets, double downs. I remembered being crushed by unexpected defeats —

good cards beaten by better cards. Hands by the book and with the book going out the window. None of it accumulated in my head. It went through, each hand a snapshot, isolated. I knew how much I'd lost, but it was too ridiculous, too farfetched to take seriously. People like me didn't lose thirty-five thousand dollars overnight — how had I even gotten my hands on that much? I was numb. I couldn't imagine what this would mean to our lives. It was crazy. What would Jewel say? What could she? I laughed when I thought of hiding it from her. Maybe we could get loans, remortgage, get work, who knew?

Suddenly I was the guy in the newspaper who loses everything at the casino. I sat in the car and looked across the garage. There were plenty of cars. It was dark. I had a headache, reached into the glove box for aspirin. There was a small bottle of isopropyl alcohol in the compartment, and I took that out, unscrewed the cap and set it on the dash. Then, carefully, I pooled a little alcohol in my palm and set the bottle down in the drink holder. I rubbed my hands together, then did their backs, the wrists, finally my face, wiping both hands over the forehead, down the nose, back across the cheeks, and under the chin to my neck. I breathed deeply so that the alcohol scorched my nostrils.

I wiped a spot that showed up under the cap on the dash, then screwed the cap on the bottle and put the alcohol away.

If I could win a couple thousand, maybe five, that would be a big improvement. That would be something. I could play conservatively, hundred-dollar bets, try to build it up over a long time. I'd done that. Or I could bet it all, win two hands and get out. I'd have to get some cash from the bank, but wasn't sure how I could do that — deposit a check from the money-market account, which was out of state, to cover some check I would write to the bank? That would work up to the amount I had in the money market, but that wasn't enough.

I sat in the car, staring out the windshield. My clothes reeked of smoke. I was wasted, my back ached, my arms ached, they were too heavy to lift. I thought about telling Jewel. I imagined myself on the side of our bed waking her up, her eyes squinting open, closing again as I told her about my night at the Paradise.

I walked rectangles on the timber piers behind the Paradise, surrounded by shrimp boats. Daylight was an unwelcome promise in the sky. Fog was thick as cotton. I was a gambler with a fistful of cash receipts and a portable phone, and I was wandering around wishing I was an architect, a husband, an ordinary guy, a middle-class Ford-Explorer-driving guy with wife, child, dog, house. A good life. But that wasn't what I was anymore, the night had seen to that. I had not imagined, months before, that it could come to this, much less would. We were going to have some fun, play the slots the way people do on vacation, lose a few hundred, leave with our heads full of triple bars and double diamonds.

I could barely see twenty feet in front of me. Bulbs on top of posts in the parking lot dropped parasols of bluish light. It was a giant auditorium out there, the size of half a city, the ceiling so high up it couldn't be found. A place you couldn't see across for the fog. What I heard was the ring and clink of pulleys and ropes on the masts of shrimp boats, the riggings. Things banging and bobbing in water, metal against metal, wood against wood. The rhythms were regular. The scene might have been pretty, is what I thought. I tried to crack my neck.

A couple of dice dealers I recognized walked across the parking lot and up the sidewalk toward the back of the casino. I waved. The guys had on their black pants and tuxedo shirts, their snap-on ties at half-mast. I had read that casinos made dealers wear pants with no pockets so they couldn't steal, but I'd checked and at the Paradise all the dealers had pockets. Craps, baccarat, blackjack, Caribbean stud — whatever the game. And they were always heartbreakingly sweet. They went to craps school if they were blackjack dealers, blackjack school if they dealt craps. They got three-ring binders from the casino — how to deal Caribbean stud, what to do if the Shufflemaster jams, how to riffle and strip cards. Without the casino they would have been high school teachers or insurance salesmen.

And since I was a regular, they were my friends, only now I couldn't bear to see them, I couldn't endure their sympathy.

On the jetty, gulls squealed and water splashed. I studied the amazing glittering mist. I was waiting for Jewel. I'd called her from the car and suggested she come see me. There was something in the way I said it. She didn't ask, didn't complain, didn't wonder if it could wait.

A graveyard cocktail waitress named Renee came out for a smoke. She couldn't have been more than twenty-four. She wasn't exactly beautiful, more like sly and disarming. Handsome. Sexy. She was tall, five ten, had a flattish face, blond crinkled hair, thin eyes, a ruby mouth, a high waist, long fingers. She looked good in the outfit — ten inches of skirt and everything else legs, black tights and high heels, a gold vest over a white dress shirt. Toy bow tie. She grinned a lot when she was working, as if she were laughing all the time, as if everything were funny to her. She had run drinks for me earlier. She was the kind of girl who might meet a winner and end up raising thoroughbreds in Kentucky.

"What are you doing out here?" she said.

"Thinking about my sins," I said. "How are you? What time is it?"

"After six," she said. "I asked where you were. Somebody said you'd gone out."

"I had a bad night."

"How bad?"

"Don't ask," I said.

"Oh. You going back in?"

"Yeah. If I can get something out of Phil or somebody. Whoever's working," I said.

"Phil's off at eight. After that it's Carlin."

Renee told me she was thinking about going back to school. She'd started college, then married a jailhouse lawyer in Florida. Nothing to write home about. "But I got out of it," she said. "I got myself over here and got the job, a place to live. So I'm doing all right."

"Good," I said. "I'm glad for you."

"I like it here," she said. "I like my place especially. It's not far, just a few blocks. They redid this sixties complex across from the beach. It's nice. Two-story, wood siding, eight units."

"Somebody sent you," I said, catching up with her.

"Well," she said. "Not really."

I thought of taking Renee and going to her apartment, locking the door, running the water, maybe a shower, sleep, television, sex. The consolation prize. Lose five thousand and they offered you a complimentary breakfast, for thirty-five you got Renee.

"I'm waiting for my wife, thanks," I said.

She looked back toward the casino, maybe a hundred yards away, then raised up and kissed my cheek. I put an arm around her waist, smoothed her skirt.

Renee slid a hand down my forearm as she walked away. "You catch me if you change your mind, will you?"

I watched her go. I figured I had ten minutes before Jewel got there. The casino was next to a marina that featured performing dolphins. I walked over there and found a flap torn in the eight-foot chain-link fence, slid in and went for a look at the pool. There were three dolphins moving like slow logs at the bottom of too blue water. We'd been to the marina, and even in daylight these weren't happy-go-lucky California dolphins. These were beat-up things that once in a while leaned out of the water under a parabolic shed covered with sprayed-on concrete that was dropping off in baseball-glove-size chunks. In the best of times these dolphins looked as if they wanted nothing more than another nap.

I sat on the edge of the ratty pool and waited for the dolphins to swim up for a look. They never came. I moved along to the other thrills of the park — the Ocean World Museum, the Society of Fish and Game Registry, the Many Wonders of the Sea Building.

When I got back to the pier behind the Paradise, I looked for Jewel, then went out another long dock where some Vietnamese were working on their boat. They were scooting around, getting ready to go out, or cleaning up after having come back, I couldn't tell which. A lot of Vietnamese played blackjack. They chattered. Maybe about the game, the dealer, the waitress — who knew? Maybe fish.

The vivid scent of shrimp was everywhere. I liked it. As a kid, whenever a skunk was around, I could never get enough. In the car, passing skunk smell on the highway, I rolled down my window while others rolled up theirs. It was a family joke. Skunk Boy, they called me.

The fog went around the pier lights like a Stephen King show, like a million moths. The boats creaked and jawed. Bits of Asian rock 'n' roll, showy and queer on some low-watt local station, cut the air. Across the water I heard the cries of birds, the slap of waves, the thud of wood against wood.

I remembered earlier, before I started playing in earnest, watching Mr. Anh, the well-dressed Asian, playing blackjack at his reserved table. He was winning. Everybody was enjoying it. The pit boss was kibitzing, telling Mr. Anh when to hit, when to double, when to stand. Mr. Anh wasn't buying the pit boss's advice. "No, no," he said. The pit would tell him to hit twelve because the dealer was showing a three. Mr. Anh would say, "No, no, no. I stand." Then he would hit a fourteen on his next spot against the same three. It was all in his head, what to do, when to hit, what would happen. And he was sweating while he played. That's what I liked best, the sweat, the way Mr. Anh perspired when things got edgy. That and the winning.

"You look like a movie of the week," Jewel said when she found me leaning against the scaling blue paint on the side of a fifty-year-old shrimp boat.

"I'm TV all right," I said.

She was wearing sweats, a light jacket, flip-flops over socks. Last night's rain had warmed things up. She walked me off the pier to her car, put me in there with Frank, then climbed up behind the wheel and took us for a drive. We were sitting high in the four-by-four, riding along the coast highway with Frank in back. It was hard to teach Frank to stay in back. Most times he rode in front, where he wanted to sit in somebody's lap. We headed for Bay St. Louis.

"Tell me," she said.

"It's big," I said.

Frank stuck his head between the seats. She drove and I talked. She moved quickly from disbelief to resignation. Then she was laughing.

"I knew you'd laugh," I said.

She stopped laughing. "It's six in the morning, Ray. You lost thirty-five thousand — we could live on that for a year. Jesus. We were six down to start with. What can I do? Is this your father dying? What the fuck are you thinking?"

"Don't know. There was a hundred thousand in the dealer's rack. I wanted some. I thought I could get it. I bet a thousand. There was so much blood pumping, my skull was hot inside, and the cards were like razors. Winner. Winner. I was up, Jewel. Forty thousand, more. Fifty. Winning was incredible, but it went like that — bang. Losing, losing was unbelievable."

"Ray?" Jewel said. "Are you hearing yourself?"

"Yes." I scratched Frank's head, which was resting across my lap.

She pulled off on the side of the road for a second, sat there staring out the windshield at nothing. I heard her breathing. "We don't have it, we don't nearly have it," she said, switching around in the seat.

"No, we don't," I said.

She slipped the car into Drive, got back on the highway. "We are fucking crazy. And *you* are craziest."

"It's the only way we can play out of our league. Where it's like, real. The pro tour, whatever. Whole thing. Real as it gets."

"That's something we want?" she said.

"Yes," I said. "Always. Everybody. Maybe the only thing we want."

We drove all the way down the coast to my mother's house, on Torch Street in Bay St. Louis, circled the block, then drove down by the beach. We stopped at a drive-in and got breakfast biscuits. I ate one and gave one to Frank. We parked a few minutes, watched gulls, watched the fog recede. Then we headed back for Biloxi.

"I'm still playing," I said.

"How did I know that?"

"That's why I called. Maybe I'll catch a few hands, undo some of the damage."

"And maybe you'll drop twenty more."

"I can't," I said. "The cards are used up, checking account's gone, they're holding markers on top."

"Everything's used up?"

"Pretty much," I said. "Maybe I can get something, a stake. There's no use pulling out now."

"Why not?"

"If it was ten, sure. But here I get five and take a shot. Lose that and we're no worse off than we are now."

"Five worse," Jewel said, but I could tell that she wasn't in the argument.

"That's what I mean," I said.

She drove the rest of the way to the Paradise without another word, pulled into the garage to let me out. I cocked the door but stayed in the passenger seat, letting my right leg swing out so that my toe scraped the concrete. She floated her fingers over my wrist.

"You floor me," I said.

"Yeah. You too," she said.

I stepped out of the car and she kissed a finger at me before she drove off.

I backed across the garage watching her go, then turned and went over the knuckled joint to the casino entrance, went through the glass doors there, listened for a few minutes to the din, felt the spongy carpet underfoot, took a breath, headed for the cashier. I had a couple of hours to kill, and needed something to kill it with.

I got home close to six that evening, having lost another eight thousand that I'd gotten partly by going to the bank for a small signature loan and partly through a boost in my credit limit at the Paradise. Jewel had dinner ready, so I cleaned up and sat down with her at the table. I was thirty-six hours without sleep, bleary, shocked.

"So," she said. "I don't know, what do *you* want to do tonight?"

"Where's RV?"

"Out. It's Friday. They're gathering at somebody's house. The usual."

Neither of us had an appetite, but both of us moved the food. The dining room had an odd, egg-shaped darkness about it. I felt as if it were closing in on us, then I shook that off and tried to think of what I could say. There wasn't anything, so that's what I said.

"You got that right," she said.

I tugged at my wallet and handed it to her. "I think I have to take a nap," I said.

"Sure," Jewel said. "Go on."

I went into the bedroom, hooked my jacket on the doorknob,

sat on the edge of the bed wondering when the screaming would start. I felt as if everything in my life had shifted suddenly, I wasn't who I was anymore, our life wasn't what it was. I counted up all the losses, from August on. It came to forty-nine thousand. That's what I got, but I could have been off by one or two. A couple checks I'd written to the casino wouldn't clear the bank.

I fell backwards onto the bed and brought my wrist up over my eyes to block out the light. I remembered a five-thousand-dollar hand I'd won, a twenty-five-hundred-dollar bet doubled down on an eleven against a king. And such relief when my face card came — like my head was cracking open. I smiled, drawn, tight, my face stiff under my wrist. I registered the twirl of the ceiling fan in changing light behind my closed eyelids and the stench of my clothes from cigarette smoke. I felt my body heave as I breathed. I was past tired, but with the headache and the fatigue I wasn't sure about sleep. I started pressing the back of my wrist against my brow, then hitting myself with the wrist, lifting it a few inches off my forehead before smacking it back down into the bridge of my nose and the ridges over my eyes. That changed the light in an interesting way. Behind my eyes I saw a black image of arm and wrist, like a cutout, surrounded by a whitish light and a dark red background, and the sound I heard was like a monster clomping through an empty wooden house. I did that for a few minutes until it became more than uncomfortable, then I stopped and listened to the thin whistle in my ears.

We went through the next week like sleepwalkers. I made some arrangements at the bank to cover the bad checks, and we had a Thanksgiving dinner that was none too happy. On Saturday morning we found a fifth of vodka in RV's backpack, but when we confronted her about it she said it was Mallory's, and for some reason Jewel and I believed her. RV was seeing Jeff regularly now, though it was a different kind of dating than any I remembered, nearly platonic.

We saw a singer on TV one night with a small diamond in her nose, and RV told us she wanted to have something like that. It sounded fine to me, but Jewel decided we should wait and be sure RV still wanted it when she was sixteen. So that was the deal we made with her — if she wanted it when she was sixteen, she could have the diamond.

"It looked good on the singer," I said to Jewel later.

"I know," she said. "That surprised me."

"I'm closing the office," I said. "Then I'll try to get something else."

"I wish it hadn't come to that," she said.

"Yeah, well, I kind of pushed it, didn't I?"

Years before, when we first got to Biloxi and I was doing well, I thought it would go on forever, that there wouldn't be a slowdown, that people would always come to me with business, that something would always turn up. For a while that wasn't far from true. A couple of times I had taken work from larger architectural firms on specific projects — office buildings, shopping centers, that sort of thing. Most of the time, however, I made it on my own, doing houses, small commercial buildings, renovations. That work dried up when the big firms came down from Philadelphia and New York to do the casinos, and brought with them lots of young architects eager to do any work they could get their hands on. I wasn't as eager anymore, and I had a reputation, so I didn't meet a lot of people who wanted me to work on their houses. That wasn't a terrible loss, because most of those people wanted to design their own. They brought doodles on legal pads and drugstore graph paper. At first I tried to talk them out of their plans, and later I made do, worked around their doodles. I'd never done a project I liked completely. Between the client's limitations and mine, that was too much to hope for. There were parts of things I'd done that I was proud of, but I took my portfolio photographs carefully. By now that didn't matter anyway. When I had work, it was as a high-paid draftsman, and I didn't have work very often, nothing since late spring. I had an idea what the outcome would be before I started calling people who ran other small shops. Nobody had work. The couple of designers I knew who were getting by were working on garage renovations. Everybody I talked to said all the new work was going out of town. It was all for the casinos, one way or the other, and they brought in their own people. I had shut down my practice before, in lean times, but doing it then had been scary, even though you could start up again with one job. This time, quitting was a relief.

On the Monday after Thanksgiving, Jewel and I went to the office, a two-room space in a house that had turned commercial. We cleaned out all my equipment, paid the last half of the month's rent and figured to lose the deposit. I called a guy named Odom and sold him most of the office equipment and furniture for a dime on the dollar. I hoped that in the worst case I might be able to get some supervision work out of him after the first of the year.

For some reason, I wanted to go out to the storage shed every afternoon, rearrange the stuff, restack the boxes. I took my mother once, because we needed to move some boxes from her house, but mostly I went alone. After a few visits I had it looking like a regular motel room. A coffee table, two or three chairs, a long set of shelves with boxes stacked on them along one side. I put some of the office equipment out there, but Jewel wanted me to set up at home.

"You can work out of the house," she said. "There's nothing wrong with that. Get that home-office tax deduction."

"I could if there was any work," I said.

"You can probably get something," she said. "Don't you imagine?"

"No," I said.

"Well, it won't hurt to try," she said.

I spent a couple days spreading my résumé around town and setting up the den off the kitchen as a part-time office, someplace I could draw if I needed to. Somebody from a building supply company called and asked if I was interested in detailing Pella wood folding doors for six dollars an hour. I said it was a kind offer and I'd have to think about it.

We took what was left in RV's college fund and paid something on each of the credit cards, to bring them down a little.

"I think this is a good idea," she said. "You stay here and design some stuff. Get back into it. Read some magazines, read some books. Do some competitions. Don't they have design competitions anymore?"

"Sure, but they're for cities and like that."

"Well, do your own city," she said. "Call it Raytown."

"I'll call it Hereafterville," I said.

"I'm serious," Jewel said. "We're O.K. We're not going to eat dirt. I'm still hanging on, keeping all the stuff in the air."

We hadn't figured out how to handle the debt. Apart from that, we thought we might be able to get by on Jewel's salary, if we didn't go overboard. Anything I made could go toward paying off the losses. But there wasn't any plan for paying off the cards and the personal loans.

"I've got some ideas," Jewel said one afternoon.

"Good," I said. "I've got some, too."

"We should compare notes," she said.

"It's a deal," I said. "When do you want to do that?"

"Later," she said. "But we have to do it pretty soon, because when the bills come in we're going to be screwed."

"The cards will just ask for a hundred and fifty dollars."

"A hundred forty of that will be interest," she said. "That's why we need to do something."

It was four-thirty in the afternoon. We were on the bed, on top of the covers, resting. Frank was there, too. Frank had been running around in the back yard, chasing everything, so now he was panting hard, shaking the bed.

"What's this magic-fingers thing he's doing to the mattress?" I said.

"He's trying to cheer you up."

"I'm cheered up fine," I said. "Nothing wrong with me a pot pie wouldn't cure."

"That's what you want for dinner?" Jewel said.

"Chicken," I said.

"You got it. I'm on my way. I'm headed for the pot pie roundup." She slid off the bed and started tucking in her shirt-tail.

"Does it seem to you that we aren't taking our situation all that seriously?" I said.

"I'm taking it seriously," Jewel said. "We're doing what can be done. How seriously do we have to take it? I mean, is this pot pie going to make you happy or what?"

"Stranger things have happened."

At three thirty-three that morning I was driving one of the Explorers in circles around the Seaside Mall parking lot, wondering how soon my mother would die. It was only the end of November, but Seaside Mall was already eyebrow-deep in Christmas. After a while I went out Highway 49 to the twenty-four-hour Wal-Mart and bought two freshly baked cake doughnuts with chocolate icing. I ate the first one in the car while leaving the parking lot. When I got back out on the highway, I took a single bite out of the second one and threw the remainder out the window. I balled up the bag and the tissue and put them on the seat beside me, then thought better of that, zipped the window down, and threw the paper out, too.

Then I shouted "Fuck you" out the window and started throwing out all the other shit I could find in the car — two magazines, a Coke can, the first aid kit, some receipts, a paperback book, a half-eaten candy bar, an old dog collar, a yellow towel, all the crap Jewel had jammed into the ashtray.

On the way home, I was going down Hochstetter Street by the Urgent Care Clinic when an asphalt-black cat walked out in front of me, crossing the street. I stopped in the middle of the block, forced a car to go around me, then backed up in such a way that the front of the Explorer was facing the direction the cat was walking, and turned around and went away from the cat and made a wide loop, six or eight blocks beyond where I'd seen the cat and in the direction of the cat's travel — all this so I could be sure the cat had not ever actually *crossed* my path.

The following week was quiet. I worked in the makeshift office or went out to the storage place, and at night I sat on the couch in front of the television and changed channels all night. Jewel was working, in and out, doing chores. RV came and went in the usual way, making a joke out of it any time we tried to find out what she was doing, where she was going, who she was going with.

"I don't know, fool," she'd say. Or she'd do a monster-like scrape across the living room, headed for the front door. "I be monster," she'd say.

I thought RV was a model of restraint. She could have been wearing dog collars and talking about how all her friends were in AA or NA. Maybe that was next year. For now, Jewel could talk to her. She'd come around, sit in the kitchen, get in bed with Jewel, go over what was happening.

She never talked to me. I'd always figured that was the way it was supposed to be, but when I thought about it, I couldn't figure *why* it was supposed to be that way. Maybe it seemed to fit the two of us. It was the only way we'd ever gotten along — a distant, playful aggression. It was fun, in its way. Reminded me of forties movies and tough-talking women. Veronica Lake, like that.

On Thursday night we had a family meeting at the dining room table. I'd spent the afternoon out at the storage place, and was still thinking about it.

"We probably should have brought my father over here," I said to Jewel. "Going out there reminds me. If he'd been over here, at least he wouldn't have gotten killed by a TV tray."

"Don't go there, Ray," Jewel said. "It's not healthy."

RV leaned on her elbow, popped her fingers against the tabletop, and said, "Why do I have to be here?"

"Because," Jewel said. "You're part of the family."

"I thought I *was* the family," RV said.

"We're all the family," Jewel said.

"We're going to talk about what happens next," I said. "You need to be here for that."

"You and Mom have already talked about it, I guess," RV said.

"A little," I said. "Not really."

"So just do it," she said. "You're not going to listen to me anyway."

"We want to know what you think," I said.

"I think I want to go to my room and pick scabs," RV said, scratching at her cheeks with her fingernails.

"Not among your options, monkey face," I said.

"I want to lose everything," Jewel said to RV. "Just get rid of it."

"Start over?" I said. I was sitting upright in the chair, my hands flat on the dining table, admiring my wife.

"Exactly," she said.

"What do you mean, everything?" RV said.

"House, cars, furniture, equipment, appliances, dishes, clothes, books, lamps, stereos, files, anything we can get a dime for at a garage sale. Everything," Jewel said.

"What about Frank?" RV said.

"We're not selling Frank," Jewel said.

"Thanks, Mom," RV said.

"We'll get rid of everything and move in with Ray's mother for a while, until we see what's what, and then we'll jump from there."

"Ray's mother? What about school?" RV said. "Mallory and all my friends? They won't want to drive to Bay St. Louis to get me. Besides, what room would I get in Grandmother's house?"

"Front or middle, up to you," Jewel said.

"Why would they mind?" I said. "It's more time with their cars."

"Are you selling all my old toys?" RV said.

"No, listen. We can keep whatever you want to keep. Right, Ray?"

"Toys are keepers," I said. "Mostly it's just your mother's junk and my junk we'll get rid of."

"What about school?"

"You stay in school where you are," Jewel said. "Besides, school won't be a problem until next year. By then, who knows where we'll be."

"Montana," I said.

"No way," RV said. "You people can go *alone.*"

"We people aren't going anywhere without you, doll," I said. "You got the make-or-break vote here."

"Maybe I could get a Vespa to get to school," RV said.

"Ahh," I said. "Probably, uh, no."

"It's not likely," Jewel said.

"I don't think I'm supposed to be hearing all this," RV said. "This isn't the kind of thing parents share with the children."

"That's the old days," I said. "These days you get everything."

"Don't want it."

"We know. That's why you get it."

"Oh hush, you two. Be quiet," Jewel said. "We can do this if everybody agrees."

"It'll be fun," I said, stroking RV's hair. "Tragic and stuff."

"Just what I want to be at my age," RV said, jerking her head like a person spasming during shock treatment. "Did you people forget what it's like being a teenager?"

"We most certainly did not," Jewel said.

"Sex and drugs," I said. "Right?"

RV shoved herself away from the table. "Oh, you are such retards. Do what you want. I'll just follow along behind you."

"Dragging your teddy bear in the dirt?"

"Yeah," RV said. "Where is he, anyway?"

In a little more than a week we managed to sell the cars, get the house on the market, sell the TVs, stereos, kitchen appliances, washer and dryer, beds, and the best of the furniture through the classifieds, and to have a full-fledged kick-out-the-jams garage sale for the rest of the possessions we were dumping. What we couldn't sell and were too sentimental to trash we put in the storage place with my father's stuff.

My mother, who knew about my disaster at the casino, though not its precise dimension, was more than pleased that we were coming to stay with her, no matter what the reason. At mid-week we started moving stuff to her house in Bay St. Louis. She cooked a big dinner. "It'll be weird," my mother said when we were cleaning up afterward. "It'll be like old times. Living with people."

"I think it'll be fun," Jewel said.

"It's not supposed to be permanent," I said.

"Hey," my mother said. "What are you, a heartbreaker? I want you to stay. I've got a thousand uses for you. Plus, you can wash to your heart's content. You can take me places in the car, get rid of the snakes next door, whatever."

We moved at the end of the week. Mother's was a three-bedroom house, but there were a couple of extra rooms, so there was enough room for everybody. My mother had a bath off her bedroom, and Jewel and RV and I would share the second full bath. The house was dark — the walls were dusty pastels, the windows had blinds and drapes, there were thick padded carpets, and the furniture was old and oversized — knobby bedposts, shoulder-high chests of drawers, gaudy polished wood. The old couple that had moved out of the Torch Street house were themselves making a new start at a retirement home, so they sold the house furnished, and my mother had kept most of what they'd left behind.

The first night we stayed there I said, "I like being here. I guess that's pathetic, but it's true."

"What's pathetic?" my mother said. "You need a place, I need company. We're family."

What I thought was that I ought to feel terrible about moving in with my mother, but I didn't, I liked it there. I felt less responsible than in my own house. That was a relief.

"This is as much my fault as yours," Jewel told me one of the first nights we spent at my mother's. We were in the front bedroom, cramped because Frank was in the double bed with us. Frank and Bosco weren't getting along, so they had to be kept apart.

"No. Not really. It's kind of you, but it's not true."

"I'm not arguing about it. We're going to do fine. We can run this deal this way. Pay stuff off. Your mother's very sweet. She likes having us."

"Probably," I said. "Takes her mind off Dad, anyway. So we're out house, cars, furniture, and appliances — did somebody finally buy the refrigerator?"

"Yep," she said. "Sold it."

"And savings is gone, Keogh and IRA, RV's money. What am I missing?"

"I borrowed against my retirement," she said. "Ten thousand. To straighten out the checkbook."

"O.K., what else?"

"Your note, some small things. We've paid what we can on the cards with what we cleared from selling stuff, and we'll make something from the house. Which, considering what was already on the cards, leaves us close to forty in the hole. I've got six in cash. We can get a car or pay MasterCard and keep driving Leona's. I figure it's easy from here. It could take a year or two, though."

"It doesn't sound too bad, does it? What's all this about tragedy? Let's hit the Paradise."

"Probably not going to happen, Ray," Jewel said.

"Yeah. I know."

We presented RV with a Vespa. I found it in a cycle shop in Bay St. Louis, and we figured it would do something to brighten her life, and we hoped it would not kill her in the bargain. Jewel came home early and took me to the cycle shop, I paid the guy, gassed up, and rode the scooter home. The Vespa was pretty beat-up, silver-blue, just like in the movies. When Mallory dropped RV off from school, the scooter was standing tall in the driveway.

RV came inside and went straight to her room. I knocked on the door. "Hey," I said. "We got something for you."

"Saw it," RV said.

"Well?"

"Thanks," she said.

"That's it? You don't want to go for a ride?"

She opened the door a crack. "Does it mean what I think it means?"

"What would that be?"

"Oh, I don't know," she said, doing dumbface. "Maybe divorce? Separation? Anything like that? A little something to keep the kid quiet?"

"Aw, sweetie," I said, hugging her while she squirmed to get away. "No, none of that. It's a bribe to get you to forgive my bad behavior."

"It's a very premature Christmas present," Jewel said. She was standing in the doorway to our room.

"Yeah," I said. "It's the ice cream after the doctor's appointment."

"You sure?" RV said.

Jewel came down the hall and we put our arms around each other. "We're tight as tonsils," Jewel said. "Don't you worry about us."

"Cool," RV said. "So let's try it out, O.K.?" She bumped me out of the way heading outside. Jewel and I followed her. RV jumped on the scooter, but I grabbed the saddle and said, "Hang on there, now. You know how to ride this?"

"Oh, really," she said. "I've ridden Randall's bunches of times. I'll go up and down the street here and show you."

Sure enough, she rode like a champ. When she pulled back into my mother's driveway she said, "I've got to get a license and a helmet, O.K.?"

"First thing," I said.

"Helmets cost," she said.

"Money doesn't matter," I said. "We're instilling the real true values in you now."

"Great," RV said. "I know the one I want. And I'm getting my navel pierced. Like when I'm fifteen. *Before* the diamond."

At one in the morning I sat in my mother's Oldsmobile in the parking lot outside the Jitney Jungle grocery where we shopped, looking at two outboard motorboats up on trailers. The store anchored one end of a small strip center. Behind the boats was a yellow rent-a-sign, the kind you put the letters on yourself. Somebody had chained it to a mailbox. It said, DEPART NOT FROM THE PATH WHICH FATE HAS YOU ASSIGNED. MED SHRIMP $5. ASST MGR WANTD.

It was so foggy I could only see half a block. Driving down the street, things faded in like in the movies — a gas station, a restaurant, a car repair shop. I'd stopped in the parking lot outside the grocery to look at these boats. One of the trailers was tipped up so that the back of the boat was dragging on the concrete. The other trailer had a new silver leg in the front with a bright black roller on it. There were rocks chocked in front of the trailer tires, and a cat sat in the bow of one of the boats.

I was trying to figure out how I could get some money together to go to the Paradise, maybe take a shot at the blackjack table. I was thinking of the one-big-bet approach. I'd mentioned it to Jewel earlier in the evening. I said I wanted to go and make one bet for ten thousand dollars on one hand of blackjack. I'd bet on the first hand of a new shoe, or a new deck, and we'd have a forty-nine-percent chance of winning.

"Is that true?" Jewel had said.

"Yes. I read it in one of your books."

"We have a fifty-fifty chance?"

"About," I said.

"If we win ten, that cuts our remaining debt by a quarter," she said, thinking it over. We were in the kitchen together at the time. I was on a stool, she was at the sink, Frank was curled up in a corner.

"You'd quit after one bet, if you won it?"

"I don't know. We'd have to decide that," I said.

"We?" she said.

"Yeah. I'm not doing this without you," I said.

"Of course not," she said. "Why would you? Will they let you bet ten thousand?"

"You have to set it up, but they'll let us. They let me before."

"You bet ten thousand dollars on one hand that night?"

"Yeah, I think. Lost the bet," I said. "I told you I was way ahead. I bet a lot. I don't remember how much, something."

"What's it like?" she said.

"It's ruthless. Completely ruthless. The cards terrorize you. Seconds stretch. It's like having the worst flu you can imagine for twenty seconds."

"Gee, that sounds great."

"If you lose, you know before the dealer uncovers. But often you think you've won and you haven't. That's not fair, that part."

"We're not doing it," Jewel said. "Forget it. We're not going over there and betting ten thousand dollars. We're in too deep."

"You're right," I said. "Probably wouldn't work."

So before I knew it, I'd decided to take a drive, and I was out in this parking lot by this grocery store. The fog was shifting, moving off, and I saw in the eastern sky a quarter-moon that looked like a perfect whitish wedge of lemon. Glowing. The edge where the rind would have been was brighter than the center. As the fog moved, it obscured the moon. First to a line around its quarter circumference, then entirely, leaving nothing but sky, silver sky.

I had to get some kind of work. Architecture wasn't going to happen. That didn't matter to me, somehow. I didn't care about that. Something had changed, something was different than it had been. I didn't care that much about money. Maybe it was my father, maybe it was playing blackjack way over the top, maybe it was both. Or maybe something had happened a while ago, and I hadn't recognized it until now. Money seemed like a bad joke. "We won't be able to eat?" I said, watching the moon reappear beyond a set of silhouetted telephone poles strung with lazy wire. The leafless trees lining the road looked like victims in a Japanese painting — gawky, awkward, limbs skidding off at all angles. Short trees, ten feet tall, wet and dark against the lighter sky.

I started the Oldsmobile, put it in Drive, let it roll forward in the parking lot. I didn't steer. I didn't have my foot on the accelerator. It felt as though I were floating. The car approached a light standard in a triangle of curbed grass, so I turned the wheel in order to miss the island. The grass beneath the light was bright green. At the far side of the lot, I could see the octagon of a stop sign, white against the dark bushes. The scabby trees all around the strip center reminded me of rubber stamps. I didn't feel bad. I thought I should, but I didn't. I wished I had the money back, but if I had it, I'd have gone to the casino.

I turned out of the parking lot, watched the haloing streetlights, stoplights. There wasn't anybody around. I was on the street alone, six lanes, three each direction, lined with lights. It was like a completely still wind tunnel. Three green stoplights suddenly turned yellow, then red. When I got close enough, they didn't have halos anymore. I waited while the left arrow went green, then yellow. Then the three lights turned green again. Coming at me from a distance, headlights.

I'd have to get a job. I wasn't going to be an architect. What would I do instead? Anything. Pay the rent. Be a father.

A piece of neon that lit a strip-center sign caught my eye. I made a U-turn in the middle of the street and headed back for my mother's. I wondered if I could do that, if that would be enough. Take care of RV, Jewel, my mother. Forget architecture, design. It would be like emptying myself of opinions. Would it be a pleasure to say, "Fine. Whatever you say," at every turn? Could I do that?

I rolled off Highway 90 onto Torch Street and slowly crept toward my mother's house, thinking of RV, who I guessed liked me more than she let on, and whom I adored. I pulled the car into my mother's driveway and sat there with the engine running, the lights off, the windows down. After a few minutes I shut the windows, turned off the ignition, and went inside, thinking of living forty years without opinions, smiling at the sweetness of that thought.

I lost a couple of jobs with architects right away. One with a New Jersey outfit that dropped me the same day they hired me when they decided they were CAD-intensive and I wasn't. Then I got on for a few days with Rollie Odom, the guy to whom I'd sold my office furniture. But Odom didn't have enough work drawing small changes into the off-the-shelf house plans he used to fulfill his clients' dreams to keep me, so quick enough, I was looking.

"I'm not doing architecture," I said to Jewel one afternoon when we were shopping at the Jitney.

"Fine," she said. "Take some time off."

"I don't think I'm mentally fit for architecture."

"Don't sweat it. What do you want to do?"

"I ought to do something different. I mean, a whole new way of life."

We passed the store manager's booth. I stopped and pointed to the Help Wanted sign. "Look. Maybe this."

Jewel laughed. "Overqualified. You wouldn't last a week."

"Assistant manager," I said. "I wonder what it pays? I could try it."

She twisted around and whispered, "I don't think it pays a lot, Ray."

"Probably not. Still, it's something. It's right here."

I applied for the job. I had to go through a kid named Harold, who was already an assistant manager, and who made it clear that he was *first* assistant manager. Harold was from Tarzana, California. He'd moved to Mississippi years before when his father went to work for NASA at the installation outside Picayune. Harold did a year at George Tyler Community College in Belhaven, then bagged it, moved to the coast, and went straight to work for Colonel Sanders. Then Jitney. Moved up from stock and checker to assistant manager in a year flat. He was nineteen.

I made an appointment to meet the manager the following afternoon.

The grocery was rundown. Jitney was a chain, but this particular one had seen better days. It was smallish, had nine aisles, and the signs and advertisements hanging from the ceiling looked as though they'd been around awhile. My mother shopped there because it was close, and we shopped there because she did.

That night at dinner my mother said, "Agribusiness, huh?"

"It's temporary," I said.

"A little south on the food chain, isn't it?" she said.

"That's true," I said.

"Well, whatever," she said. "I thought you might be designing us a compound, you know? Something we could build? Some way to use all the money in the estate."

That was odd. It had been weeks and not a mention of the estate, the will, nothing. I knew my father had left everything to her, but I'd expected her to want to talk to me about it. She hadn't.

"You want to build the Kaiser compound?" I said.

"I'm for it," Jewel said. "No inbreeding, though."

"We don't have anybody to inbreed," I said.

"You and me," Jewel said.

"Anything's possible," my mother said. "Bosco and Frank are O.K. They were together all afternoon and not a peep out of them."

"I guess that's a sign," I said.

"Frank's been repaired," Jewel said.

"Amen, and amen," my mother said.

I got up. "I've got to go learn the Jitney Jungle song before tomorrow," I said, going for the bedroom.

"That's a retail tycoon in the making," Jewel said to my mother. "Always a step ahead."

At the grocery the next day, I was waiting to see the manager when Harold stuck his head in to give me a preview. He said Clo Hurd was a thirty-something guy, short, stumpy, clumsy, and slow. According to Harold, Clo's father was medium high in corporate Jitney.

Clo's office was a mess, a crummy storeroom in the back with a steel desk and stacks of paper around. There were flats of canned foods and eight-by-eleven Jitney Jungle "Store of the Week" plaques on the wall. Clo stood tall in that room, peeping out into the store through the mirrored glass.

"You're overqualified," Clo said when I got settled in a folding chair. "Call me Clo."

"Everybody's overqualified for something, Clo," I said. "I can help out. I can do an honest day's work."

"Sign's been out there three weeks, and you're my first application." He looked at my résumé. "This is a silly résumé to show me for this kind of a job, isn't it?"

"Well, maybe," I said. I reached across the desk. "Here. Give it back."

Clo held up a hand. "Now wait a minute. What's the deal? How come you're nosing around a grocery? Can't get no architecture business? What happens when the mayor wants a house — where's that leave me?"

"You got a mayor over here?"

"We got the whole shooting match," Clo said. "Mayor. Council. Courts. You a drinker? Women? What?"

"I lost some money at the casino," I said. "Over in Biloxi."

"Uh-huh," Clo said, nodding big. That was the explanation he'd been looking for. "What about reliable? You're not a guy who goes off on a bender, are you?"

"Nope. I quit gambling. Moved over here to live with my mother, get straightened away. I don't figure to make the grocery business my life's work, but right now I'm taking stock, know what I mean? I need something while I get my feet under me."

"This is crap work," Clo said. "Run a register, fetch carts, stock, broom and mop. You do everything in a job like this. None of it joyful."

"I can probably handle that," I said.

A few days later I was legitimately employed. Since I'd never worked in a grocery as a kid, the whole game was new to me, I didn't know the first thing. Clo's idea was that I should do a little bit of everything, just to get in the swing of it, so I was fronting the canned vegetables on aisle seven when Harold came by and said, "You know, I have this idea."

"What is it?"

"I can trust you?" he said.

"What?" I said. "What kind of idea are you talking about?"

"We ought to get Clo," he said. He wagged a can of beets at me. "Get him fired. What do you think?"

"Get him fired?" I said. "Why?"

"You and me take over," Harold said. "Simple as that."

"He's the boss man," I said. "I'm just out here shucking peas."

"O.K.," Harold said. "O.K. Maybe that's a bad idea. What if we canned him instead? Cut him up in pieces, put him up like fruit, you know? There's a meat saw in back."

Harold was exactly the kid I was afraid RV might meet someday. He wasn't bad looking, in a football way, had a head of hair like a catalog model and a deadly smile. And he was dumb as death.

He was excited about his new idea. "I seen this film on TV. They cut off people's hands and feet, arms and legs. We're going to need big old cans for arms."

"Use the grinder," I said, figuring that the best way out of this was straight ahead. "You can turn him into hamburger meat."

"What about Margie?" Harold said.

Margie was one of the checkers, a good-looking girl, everyone's favorite. Just out of high school and had that am-I-fourteen-or-am-I-thirty? look going. A face full of fresh skin and freckles. Her uniform was always clean, pressed, sexy. The skirt part was so smooth over her backside.

"What about her?" I said.

"I burn inside for Margie," Harold said. "That's what."

Just at that minute Clo and Margie turned onto aisle seven together, walking arm in arm. Clo stopped her. They were ten feet away. Clo said, "Now here's my boys, ain't that pretty? They're working hard. I do like to watch men work."

Margie was embarrassed, and smiled a hello to Harold and me.

Clo put one hand up against a shelf, disturbing the corned beef hash. "Look at you guys skittering about there," he said. "You look like a couple of gerbils going around and around in that cage."

"Hey, Clo," Margie said. She gave him a play slap on the shoulder. "Let's go on, O.K.?"

"I *wish* I was a gerbil," Harold said, giving Margie a not subtle once-over.

"We're working hard here," I said. "Doing the job. We're smoking these cans."

"That's good," Clo said. He put his arm around Margie's waist, around the white plastic belt that cinched the pale pink shirtwaist uniform, and guided her between Harold and me.

We watched them go down the aisle. When they got next to the Libby's at the very end, Clo let his hand slip down over Margie's butt. He didn't have to turn around to know we were watching.

Harold said, "He's going to do her, right now."

"Don't be silly," I said.

"He's taking her back to his office. He's going to tear her apart. He does it all the time."

"C'mon," I said. "You got your imagination running away with you there, Harold."

"Head checker's got a price," he said. "I'll show you if you want me to."

"Nope. Thanks," I said. "Got to work."

I went back to straightening the canned vegetables. It was only my second day on the job, but I already liked it. It was soothing in a curious way, maybe because everything was so simple. The pay wasn't good, but it was enough to use the way Jewel and I had planned to use anything I earned.

Harold watched me work the shelves. He even did a little work himself. But when he came to the small white round potatoes, he decided he needed some more of those from the stockroom. "I'm going to the back," he said.

"What for?" I said.

"Potatoes." Harold dusted his hands on the seat of his pants.

"Plenty of potatoes on the flat there," I said, pointing to a red handtruck I'd brought out from the stockroom earlier.

"Got to go in the back," he said. "And if I see anything while I'm hunting potatoes, well, be that as it may."

"C'mon, Harold," I said. "Don't be a jerk."

"I ain't doing nothing." He did an awkward dance toward the back and started singing the Mr. Clean song, but he had trouble remembering the details, so he repeated the "Mr. Clean, Mr. Clean, Mr. Clean" refrain and did a big fairy-like sweep down the aisle.

I got off the overturned red plastic milk crate I'd been sitting on and watched him go. This was a problem. I liked the store, the simplicity of things, the people. It was easy and new, like I was a kid again. And I liked staying at my mother's with Jewel and RV, liked how things seemed in order. It was as if I'd retired, or was recuperating from war injuries — nothing much was asked of me. No worries. I liked going shopping with Jewel at Cowboy Maloney's Electric City out on Pass Road. I liked just about everything, and watching this beanpole kid dance toward the back of the store, I got nervous because I figured it was my responsibility to stop him from screwing things up. Maybe if I stayed out of it Clo wouldn't come after me, but I couldn't be sure. Besides, Clo had been decent enough with me — there was no reason to get on his case.

For a while I stuck with the shelves, working the black-eyed peas and the shoepeg corn. Then I got too nervous and went after Harold.

I found him in the narrow, dark-paneled hallway leading to Clo's office, doubled over and peeking into the room through the hole where the second door lock had been. Without turning around, Harold waved an arm, telling me to stay quiet, stay quiet.

"Let's get out of here," I whispered.

Harold flattened his palm over the hole and turned. "This is exactly like that *Red Shoe Diaries* show," he said. "He's wonking her right here. She loves it."

"C'mon, Harold," I said. "Leave them alone. They can do what they want to do."

"No way. You're an old married guy. Get out there and rack them cans."

I put a hand on Harold's shoulder, gave a tug, but he didn't budge.

"You're making too much noise," he hissed. He bent down to the hole again, and pretty soon he was making grunting sounds as if in time with what he was seeing. I leaned against the paneling and slid down the wall.

"C'mon, Harold," I said.

"What, you're not going to look?"

"No. Jesus Christ."

"Gimme a dollar," Harold said.

"You're charging me a dollar to quit?" I said.

"Get that dollar out here," Harold said, grinning. He held his hand out and went back to the door lock, pressing his face against it. "Oh, baby," he said. "Oh baby, oh baby, oh baby."

I took a bill from my wallet. The compressor on the big freezer compartment on the other side of Clo's office kicked on, and everything in the place started to rattle and hum.

"They're going round the world," Harold said.

I grabbed Harold's shoulder, shoved a dollar into his hand, but he wasn't giving up this part.

"Price's going up," Harold whispered.

I yanked at him and couldn't pry him loose, but then, suddenly, he gave up the hole, leaned back against the wall, and shivered all over. "Holy Jesus," he said. "Hang on a minute. Maybe they'll go again. Gimme another dollar."

"I ain't giving you squat," I said. "Let's get out of here."

Harold got up, rubbing his eyes with his thumbs, and followed me. "O.K.," he said. "So what about cutting Clo into parts? Hang him over the butcher's saw and buzz his leg? Would that be cool?" He made a sloppy buzz sound. "I can hear the saw stripping through his skin, hitting the bone, blood showering out, jetting off. Or getting his hand, running an arm through there like a two-by, zipping off a hand. He'd be squealing then."

"Why don't we do our jobs and forget it," I said. "You're going to get your ass caught if you don't watch out."

"I wouldn't mind sawing him in half," Harold said. "Not her, though. I mean, I'll do her, but I ain't sawing her. She's too fine."

I turned to face Harold, who was behind me in the hall. "You're a wanker, Harold."

"A what? Never mind, I'm gone." Harold limped past me down the hall.

I cut left and went around to the refrigeration room. I broke open a carton of ice cream sandwiches, peeled one, and ate while I waited for Clo and Margie to clear the area.

I had lunch with Harold and Margie at the McDonald's by the gas station out on the corner of the shopping center. We sat in a booth by the window, watching the cars go by. Margie was as happy as could be. She waved a french fry at me and said, "The fruitcake tells me you were watching."

"Oh, Jesus," I said to Harold. "No. I didn't see anything."

"I seen it all," Harold said.

"You mean you didn't see me and Clo in his office?" Margie said.

"No, I didn't," I said. "I didn't even look. I went back there to get dog boy here, and that's it."

"You're such a sweetie," she said.

"I got a dollar out of him," Harold said. He giggled. "He paid me a dollar to leave."

"What is that? A declaration of love?" Margie said.

"He's got a daughter," Harold said. He looked like a giant basketball player in that yellow kid's booth in the McDonald's.

"That's not it," I said. "My daughter's younger. I just figured, well, privacy, you know? Whatever you want to do."

Margie smiled real prettily, like a grown woman will. "Well, it *is* a declaration of love," she said. "What do you know."

Jewel covered her eyes when I told her the story of Clo and Margie. "O.K., that's enough for me," she said. "Thanks. Gotta run. Call soon. You finished?"

"I don't know," I said.

We were in bed. Jewel pulled the blinds up to let in the street light. "You want to stay here or what?" she finally said.

"It's fine with me. What about you?"

"It's strange," Jewel said. "Some burden is gone, something I felt all the time. Not a bad thing, but whatever it was is gone. It feels real homey over here. More than our house."

"Got the grandmother on site," I said. "That tends to correct everybody's behavior."

"I feel closer to your mother than I ever did. As if we're in the same family now, not separate families. Your mother is so sweet, she's like an angel scooting around. Like she doesn't take any space at all."

"She is an angel," I said, reaching to wrap my hands over the top of the elaborate headboard.

"So what job are you getting next?" Jewel said.

"What're you, mind reader?" I said. "You amaze me." I released the headboard and rolled to face her, resting my head on her shoulder.

"Your head weighs a ton," she said.

"Thirteen pounds," I said. "I weighed it one time."

"Big," she said. "Big-headed man. I'm writing a country song about you."

"Guess I'll call the Pella people, remember them?"

"Sure," she said.

"It won't be so bad," I said.

Late the next afternoon I was stretched out on the shiny green velour sofa looking at the TV when RV came in from riding her Vespa.

"What're you watching?" RV said.

"Nothing," I said.

"You appear to be watching this television over here," she said, wiggling her head toward the Sony.

"Perhaps things are not as they appear," I said. I was on my stomach on the couch. RV looked windblown. She wore three shirts, one seersucker, and carried a way-too-big crash helmet covered with gaudy purple graphics. The helmet was dangling from her hand, weighing her down on that side. She stared at the television, which was showing a picture of old passenger airplanes, with an inset picture of a furry animal crawling around on the rocks near a stream. I was punching up still pictures from the other channels on two sides of the screen.

"How many eyes you got?" she asked.

"Forty," I said. My voice was muffled because I was talking into the pillow.

"Where's Frank?"

"Probably on your bed," I said.

"Where's my mother?" she said.

"Work."

"Where's *your* mother?" RV took a couple of steps and sat down jerkily on the arm of the sofa. I pulled my feet out of her way.

"Went for chicken."

"Nuggets?" RV said.

"Didn't tell me."

"You want to know what Mallory did? She told Royal she wasn't seeing him again, and then, like, right in front of everybody, she started coming on to Markie. She's such a bitch."

"Uh-huh," I said, turning to look at RV. "I told you that a long time ago."

"Sure you did," she said.

"I did," I said.

It was murky in the living room. The blinds were three-quarters closed and the skies outside were overcast, so there wasn't much light. The TV color looked aggravated by having all the stills frozen on the screen. There were pictures of police, weather maps, people hunting for something in a field, an irate short man with bristly hair, a senator from somewhere. The window air conditioner rattled, stuffing the bungalow with damp, cool air.

"Why is this on?" she said. "It's winter outside."

"I'm changing the air," I said.

"You're getting a lot of shrimp smell in here," she said.

"Where'd you get the hat?" I said.

"I borrowed it," she said, spinning the helmet into the air as if it were a basketball. She caught it heading for the kitchen. "It's way pimped, huh?"

"Throw me some chips or something," I said.

"No way, dude," she said.

I was flicking the picture-in-picture back and forth, so I was picking up sound from different shows. On the mammal show

I caught somebody saying, "Beaver lodge, my home. Not only my home, but the home of my beaver people."

"C'mon," I said.

"You're so skanky," she said from the kitchen. "There are no longer any chips."

"What've you got?" I said.

She stood in front of the kitchen cabinet, a hand on each of the small doorknobs. "Oreos, gum, animal crackers — *the endangered collection* — Crazy Dough, Twizzlers."

"Oreos," I said. The air conditioner, a fat old brown Fedders with a dusty grille in the dining room window, did a triple clunk and cut off with a hissing sound. RV half shut one of the cabinet doors and looked into the dining room at the air conditioner.

"Is that thing O.K.?"

"That baby's older than you are," I said.

"It has the cheese disease," she said. She grabbed the bag of Oreos, stripped off the rubber band, took a cookie out, and ate it as she brought the bag back. "You think we'll stay here long?"

"What, you don't like it?"

"It's O.K., I guess. People think it's bad, living with my grandmother," she said.

"Oh yeah? Like who?"

"Mallory," she said.

"You said Mallory was a bitch," I said.

"So? What's your point?" RV said, handing me the bag.

A thin stream of sun cut between the blinds of one of the windows, suddenly brightening the room. Gritty dust circled in the light.

"This room kind of glows," RV said. "Reminds me of *X-Files.*"

"Lots of stuff reminds you of *X-Files,*" I said.

"Got that right," she said, reaching down to get another cookie out of the bag. "You know, I'm going to be sixteen pretty soon."

"You gotta be fifteen first."

"I will." She swiveled toward the television set, sat down on the floor with her back against the sofa.

"In the way," I said.

"You aren't watching," she said.

"I started watching after you came."

"Did not."

I shoved her aside by the shoulder. Her hair was a new shade of red, short, kind of hacked off on one side. The neck was pale and thin. She wore glasses with black rims.

"Is Grandmother going to support us forever?" she said, gnawing the icing off half an Oreo.

"She's not supporting us," I said. "We're just living with her."

"Duh," RV said. "Do you love me more than life itself?"

"Kinda do," I said.

"Well, will you go get me a pizza?"

"I can't. I promised my mother I'd stay here and watch the house," I said.

"Lies," RV said.

Mother arrived with a fifteen-piece box of Popeye's, a quart of mashed potatoes, a quart of coleslaw, a pint of gravy, and nine biscuits.

"How are you, darling?" she said, dusting her fingers over RV's new hair. She went into the dining room and put the food on the table.

"I am too tough," RV said. She got up and followed her grandmother, started unpacking the dinner, setting the table with paper towels for place mats and paper towels for napkins.

"How's young Lochinvar over there?" my mother said.

"He's great," I said.

"He watching a show about beavers," RV said.

"Beaver people," I said.

My mother was wearing slacks and a sweater. "I'm thinking of getting a job as a dealer, what do you think?" She brought two bottles of beer out of the kitchen and put them alongside the place RV had made for her at the head of the table.

"Great idea," I said. "Complement my grocery income."

"Why don't *you* get a job as a dealer?" she said.

RV brought strawberry preserves out of the kitchen and sat down. I stuck it out on the sofa.

"I like my chicken cold," I said.

"He would, wouldn't he?" she said to RV.

"He wouldn't get me a pizza," RV said. She had one leg folded under her, and she sat up and leaned over the table so she could see into the box of chicken. "You want the breast part or the thigh part?"

"Thigh," my mother said.

RV fished chicken out of the box and dropped it on her grandmother's plate. We used high-quality paper plates — Chinet brand.

"He's never getting off the couch, and he's never answering my question, is he?" my mother said.

"He's been stuck there since I got home," RV said.

"At least it's not MTV."

"I'm watching that later." I groaned and rolled off the couch, landing on my knees by the coffee table. Then I went in and took a drumstick out of the box and began eating it as I stood by the table, looking at the Fedders. "I thought about that dealer thing," I said.

"Yeah? What'd you think?"

"Probably not," I said. "It's a good living, though, tips and everything. Anyway, RV's getting married."

"She is?" my mother said.

"She's serious about the new guy."

"All lies," RV said.

"Fine with me," my mother said. "Where're you all going to live?"

"Here," RV said. She looked at her grandmother, then me. "I don't think anything has to change. Do you, Dad?"

I staggered. "She called me *Dad*. I don't know what to do. The second time in fourteen years."

"Is not," RV said, wagging a chicken leg at me. "You haven't even known me fourteen years. And I call you Dad all the time."

"Never did," I said.

"Well, you're Dad in my head," RV said.

My mother had a hooked piece of fried chicken skin caught on the side of her lip. "No marriage before sixteen," she said. "House rules."

Mother went to take a nap before work. I read a magazine, and then about six-thirty RV came in and told me she wanted to show me this place she'd found. "It's someplace we could live or something," she said.

"You're really into this moving business, aren't you?"

"No, it's just a place. I'll take you out there," she said.

"I'm driving the scooter," I said.

"Don't call it that," she said.

We got on the Vespa and rode a couple of miles inland on Engel Avenue to a place called Lake Forgetful, shielded from the road by giant hundred-foot pines. The lake was small, a pond of maybe five or six acres, with a trailer park built around one end. On the road leading to the trailers there was a visitors' parking area with room enough for six cars. That's where I put the Vespa. There were ducks on the water and a few lights in the tall pine trees that surrounded the lake, which, in the dark, looked shiny and calm. We walked around the water in one direction, then turned and walked around in the other direction.

"This is so cool," RV said.

"You want us to get one of these mobile homes up here?" I said, pointing up toward the trailers.

"Sure," she said.

It was great being out there with her, something new, like we were pals, still jockeying for position but definitely aligned with each other, happy to be friends. We went arm in arm, and she looped a hand up on my shoulder. I felt the curve of her waist beneath the shirts.

"You trying to shake my mother?" I asked.

"No, she's cool," RV said. "She can come. But I found this place and it is so great."

"What do you mean, you found it?"

"I *found* it," she said. "Kids come out here sometimes to hang." She swung around in front of me, walked backward, matching her steps to mine. She held her arms out as if to showcase the area, then said, "You know. Kids."

"Oh," I said.

She stopped and waited for me to catch her, then said, "This is where I had my first kiss. Well, my first *real* kiss, anyway."

I swung my arms up as if to protect my face from a blast. "No, please! Don't tell me, don't tell me. I don't want to know. We ain't buying anything out here. I have to go."

"Oh, settle down," RV said.

"Why are you telling me this?" I said. "Yikes. Two months ago we were grounding you for alcohol abuse."

"I've matured a lot since then," RV said. "You've probably noticed."

"Last I noticed, you were carrying contraband vodka," I said.

"That was Mallory's."

"I know," I said. "We believed you."

"You'd better," she said.

A moon was sliding up behind the pines. It filled the clearing over the lake with vanilla light. Cars fizzed by on the road. There was some dinky music coming from the trailer park. Pine needles everywhere.

"I'll bet these things cost next to nothing," RV said. "We could buy two or three. Put 'em in a circle. It'd be so great to be out here all the time."

"They cost plenty," I said.

"You and Mom could have a baby," she said. "Like Frank, only it would talk."

"Wouldn't have enough legs," I said. "So, who'd you kiss? And when, and everything. And how come you've matured so much?"

"I gave up drinking, mostly. I smoke a little weed sometimes."

"You do," I said, throwing a twig I found into the water. "Where do you smoke weed?"

"Cars, mostly, Dad. Dead ends. Cul-de-sacs. We go down there to hang and talk. It's just weed, anyway. It won't hurt you."

An owl hooted in a tree somewhere. Leaves rustled. The water lapped uncertainly at the edge of the lake. Lights winked on and off in the trailer park to our right. A screen door slammed as some people came outside. They were laughing, walking toward us.

"Uh, there's a person," RV said, pointing to our right, at the trailer park. We stopped and looked toward the sounds. We were almost directly across the water from the trailers. Two figures stepped out of the pines, out of the darkness, and stood at the lake's edge, laughing.

One man said, "Why is heroin better than a woman?" His voice was crystal clear. Like perfect radio reception.

The other said, "Huh?"

"Why is heroin better than a woman?" the first one repeated.

The second one laughed. Then with a rush, we heard one of the men pissing into the water, then the other started.

"So that's how they do it," RV said in a whisper.

"Shh," I said.

"Well?" the first guy said.

"I don't know. I give up," the second guy said.

"C'mon," the first guy said. "Guess." They both laughed more and finished up pissing, then started back for the trailers.

"Ah, dudes," RV whispered. "Come on. What's the answer?"

When the men were gone, she and I skirted the end of the lake, crunching through the noisy grass. When we got to the parking spot, RV made an elaborate business of getting into her helmet — she smacked herself a couple of times in the head, readjusted the chin strap, grabbed the helmet with both hands, and wiggled it until she was comfortable. She looked ready for space travel.

"I'm driving," she said, swinging a leg over the seat.

"O.K.," I said, climbing on behind her.

She punched the engine to life and twisted the scooter around, settling on the seat and bouncing. I duck-walked until she gave it the gas and we shot out from under the high pines, away from Lake Forgetful. We went back into town and rode the beach highway toward home, me with my arms around her tiny waist. She was singing as she drove. There was a lot of wind. Sleek and mysterious cars zoomed by us. Lights sparkled out over the Gulf. I kissed the back of that flashy helmet, sure that she would never know.

The next day Margie was especially perky behind her register, chatting and laughing with the customers as she pinged the bar codes over the reader. I was all over the store, working the shelves, the stock, mopping the back, sacking for Margie. Clo was gone most of the afternoon but returned around five, manned a register during the dinner rush, then, when things started slacking off, went back to his office. By seven-thirty the place was dead. I worked the produce section, doing what I could to make the bananas, apples, and oranges look as if they were happy. I left Harold over there watering things down and went up to the front where I caught Clo and Margie chatting.

"Hey, Ray. How's it hanging?" Clo said.

"Be here now," I said.

Clo held his hands out to his side and shook his head as if he didn't get it. Then he turned to Margie. "Let's take a trip, what do you say?"

"I'm tired, Clo," Margie said. "It'll keep."

He jangled his keys. "I don't know. I think the boss is ready to go."

She patted his shoulder and smiled. "You give him a big hug

for me. I'm getting my stuff and getting out." She dodged around Clo and headed for the back. "Howdy, Ray," she said.

Clo turned. "Ray? You finished in produce?"

"Harold's handling it," I said.

"You mop eight and nine?" Clo said.

"Sure did," I said.

"New milk out?" Clo said.

"Yes sir," I said.

"How about you head out front and round up them baskets then," Clo said.

"Got 'em already," I said, waving toward the front windows where the carts were packed solid.

"Shoot," Clo said, heading after Margie. "Well, just hang around until the ball drops, O.K.?"

"Clo?" I said. "Can we talk a minute?"

"Can it wait, Ray?"

"Not really," I said. "Now's the time."

Clo straightened the rack of tabloids. "All right," he said. "What is it?"

"Well, this is kind of my last day," I said.

He was surprised. "Already? You get something else?"

"No, I just figured this isn't for me," I said.

"Well, I can respect that," Clo said. "A man needs to know his limitations."

"That's right," I said. "And there's something else I wanted to say."

"What's that, Ray?" Clo said.

"It's about power," I said. "You know? Authority. A little bit of authority is a dangerous thing. You don't want to take advantage of it, you know what I'm saying?"

"Uh-huh," Clo said.

"You don't want to lean on it," I said. "It has a way of coming back and biting you when you least expect it."

"Right," Clo said. He was eyeing me, not quite sure what I

knew. That seemed to trouble him for a second, then he shook it off. "Gotcha. Everything's fine, Ray. You want to take off early tonight?"

"No," I said. "I'm good."

"Great," Clo said. He grabbed the microphone and switched on the PA at the register. "Harold, come to the front, please. Harold, to the front."

I looked up at the ceiling, at the white-painted corrugated metal and bar joists and air-conditioning ducts. Sometimes a bird or two lived up there. It was always a mystery to me how a bird could get in. Harold had explained that when customers complained about a bird in the store, he had to chase the bird out. Once Clo brought a BB rifle, and he and Harold had taken turns shooting at a bird until they popped the glass on a case back in meat. Then they tried herding it out, propping the doors open and running through the store with brooms, throwing things at the ceiling where the bird was sitting on one of the joists.

When Harold emerged from the produce section, Clo said, "Watch the front, will you, Harold?"

Then he put an arm around my shoulders and started walking me toward the rear of the store. "You know, Ray," he said, "there's something you ought to understand. Nobody's getting hurt here. You shouldn't get upset because I have a bit of good fortune. See, you've got all kinds of possibilities. In a month or two you'll be dancing at the yacht club, but I'm a grocery store manager. I've got a junior college degree, and I'm paying for a couple of kids who don't like me much, and I can't sleep. At three o'clock this morning I was up watching *Lingerie Dreams II* on pay-per-view. And I'm a churchgoing man, so watching that made me feel ugly. But we do these things anyway, know what I'm saying? Don't know why, don't seem to have much choice. So you look at my situation one way, and maybe I'm taking advantage of my authority here at the store. Look at it another way, and I'm a loser being treated kindly by a generous fellow traveler. That's the way I like to frame it."

"I hadn't thought of that, exactly," I said.

"Well," Clo said. "Now you have. Thanks so much for working with us here at Jitney." He patted my shoulder, gave me a strong handshake, and then turned to go back to his office. I stopped in the middle of the aisle, in front of the packaged meats, idly straightening some rib-eye steaks and some filets, some strip steaks, some boneless cuts.

I called Cohen Associates, the Pella folding-door people, to see if the job they'd called me about was still open. It was. I interviewed and got it. It was a nothing job detailing special wood folding doors and windows, and commercial toilet enclosures, for a company that supplied them to builders. Pella had been manufacturing the stuff for years. Contractors and builders had a big markup, so they liked to use them, and it was up to the supplier, Cohen Associates, to provide the detailed working drawings for installation. My job was to sit at a drafting table in a wood-paneled office and trace details from one set of drawings to another, redoing the dimensioning, the furring, cranking the stuff out. Cohen had the same arrangement with a manufacturer of toilet enclosures, so I did those, too.

The office was in another strip center off the interstate, where the highway curled down toward the beach, and my employer was a mouse-like guy named Art Cohen. This guy was five feet tall and ran a family-owned plumbing and building-supply business that had been operating in Bay St. Louis for three generations. My part with them was a sidelight, something to keep certain manufacturers happy.

"I also got a car wash business," Art told me the first week I was there. "I give it to my son, Willard. He runs it. He thinks it's fun. He's a man who loves water. You should go out there sometime and give him some business."

So that night Jewel and I took the Oldsmobile out to see Art's car wash. We hadn't bought a car, hadn't even decided whether we were going to or not, but we were going to need something soon.

I recognized Willard Cohen, Art's son, before he recognized me. He was the guy I'd met at the casino the first time Jewel and I went, Winky Cohen, new husband of Baby. He was big, maybe six six, three hundred pounds, not fat but not Mr. Olympia either. Just plain big. When he handled things — oil cans, trash barrels, crates — everything looked light as a feather. Pencils shrunk in his hand.

"Well, howdy," he said when I reminded him about the Paradise. "I remember. You were losing, right?" He had "Winky" embroidered on the oval name badge on his shirt.

I introduced Jewel and explained the connection. She said she'd met him, but he didn't remember.

"I'm sorry," Winky said. "You get over there and all hell breaks loose. You never know which way things are going to go."

"I've just started working for your father," I said.

"Is that right? What do you do over there?"

"Draw. I used to be an architect."

"I was going to say you didn't look much like warehouse trash to me."

"I do the detailing on the working drawings," I said. "Pella doors, windows, and I do the bathroom fixtures."

"Oh," he said, grinning. "You're the new stall man. Jesus, is that the worst job or what? Sit there all day drawing toilet stalls."

"I haven't done too much yet," I said. "Just starting."

"It'll come," Winky said. "He does a lot of business in toilet enclosures. I had to work for him one time when I dropped out of college. Nothing worse. This out here is a dream compared to that, I'm telling you."

"So how's, uh, your wife?"

"Baby? She's great. She couldn't be better. She's been over there at the Paradise nonstop since we saw you. Won thousands of dollars. Hit twenty-five thousand once, can you believe that?"

"Twenty-five?" I said. "Shit."

"Yeah, she did," he said. "It's great stuff. You still going over there?"

I held up my hands. "Nope. I kind of gave it up."

"I know what you mean," he said. "Some people have it, some don't. I never won diddly over there. But Baby, why, she's a born winner."

"So you just run this out here, huh?" I said.

"Yeah, it's fine. We couldn't get a car clean if our lives depended on it, but nobody cares. I gotta watch the garbage I hire to scrub the wheels and wipe the cars down after they come through the Hogan. That's what we call the wash tunnel over here," he said, gesturing toward the back of the building. "That's not what it is, really. We replaced the Hogan two years ago. Hogan is one of those felt and spray jobs. We got a new deal where nothing touches the car, nothing. Easy on the finish."

"So you run this for Art?"

"You know, that's not clear. Sometimes it's mine, sometimes it's his. Depends on how he feels, really. He gave it to me, but then he took it back. Now he gives it back to me every once in a while. It runs itself, really. I'm the baby-sit boy. I just sit out here and read and collect the money."

We ran the Olds through the wash and Winky wouldn't take a nickel for the job his guys did. He was right about not getting the car clean. We shook hands again, he gave me a card, we said goodbye and that we'd see each other soon.

"He's a big fella," Jewel said on the drive home.

"I like him," I said.

"Me too," she said. "That's what I mean."

"We can add him to our circle, then," I said. "We can take Winky and Baby out to dinner sometime."

"Sure," she said. "After the first of the year. After we get through Christmas."

"We got Christmas dead ahead," I said.

"That's it," Jewel said.

"We'll get ourselves a car for Christmas. What do you say?"

"It's good for me," she said. "We can bring it out here and wash it all the time. Maybe go bowling. He looks like a guy who could bowl. You know how long it has been since I went bowling?"

"Way too long," I said.

We celebrated my first week at Cohen Associates with a dinner at the Lady Luck casino. Jewel and RV and I were supposed to meet there at nine, but I was early, playing quarter slots, and then, after eight, going outside to watch the fire-breathing-dragon show. The Lady Luck had built a garage-size warehouse in the water outside the casino, put a lot of chicken wire on it, then sprayed it with blow-on concrete, and painted that to look like a huge rock by Mattel. Every night at six-thirty and eight-thirty they had this little drama with Oriental music, smoke, and thunder, and then the rock opened up and the fire-breathing dragon came out and roared at the crowd.

I leaned on the thick red pipe railing, and when a clean-enough-looking woman came and stood about ten feet away I smiled and said, "Winner or loser?"

"Who's asking?" she said, without even turning to look at me.

I liked that, liked it that she spoke straight out into the wind in front of her, made no effort to be sure I heard, did not care what I looked like — wasn't even interested enough to glance.

"Loser asks," I said. "I was up, but — you know."

Now she looked. She had straight black hair in a kind of bowl cut, a body stocking, miniskirt, black jacket, black boots laced on brass eyes.

"You look like a loser," she said.

I looked down at myself — jeans and a polo shirt. "Yeah, well, you look like a comic book. What do you think of this dragon?"

"He's big and he's bad," she said. "You want to shoot over here and get something?" She vaguely indicated the casino.

"Probably not," I said.

"Might bring you some luck," she said. "Have a couple of drinks, check the action. That's my job in life, bringing you the action."

"I'm catching the dragon," I said.

"I can wait." She lit a smoke and turned away from the dragon, looking back across the inlet between the Lady Luck and its six-story parking garage. "My name's Patti," the girl said. "I work here."

"Oh yeah? Lady Luck?"

"Yeah. I sling drinks. I saw you in there dicking with the tiny slots. You're not big money, are you?"

"Little money," I said. "But I'm a swell guy in every other way."

"What's that mean?" she asked me.

"Means I've got about half a job, I don't smack women, I clean up after myself. You know, Cary Grant."

"My luck," she said, flicking her cigarette into the army-green water. "Listen, I gotta get in costume and do a half-shift, nine to two. You want to see me after?"

I squeezed my thumb and forefinger at the bridge of my nose. "Like to," I said. "But, no."

"Wife and kids?"

"Kid," I said. "Wife and kid."

She nodded. "Yeah, well, I ain't hitting you that hard."

"It's fine. Any other time," I said.

"If things were different, you mean."

"Right," I said.

"You're a puppy," she said.

"I guess. Most times it's easy. I don't get a lot of offers."

"That's *all* I get," she said, nicking the railing with her key chain. "Twenty-four seven."

Big dragon music was coming up, tinkle and gong, monster drums, nasal song, and smoke started to roll out from under the garage-size you-paint-'em fake rock. Families were gathered around on the walkways, fathers itching to get back to their machines or tables, but pulled out to watch the display by wives who were ready to leave.

Jewel and RV came up behind me. "Hey, it's Dad the Gambler," RV said, making gang signs at me.

"You go deaf?" I said.

"That's cool," she said. "I get it."

"How's the wage earner?" Jewel said, kissing me, putting an arm around my waist, threading her thumb through one of my belt loops.

"My name is Raymond Kaiser and I lost fourteen dollars on the slot machines before you arrived," I said.

By now the dragon had rolled all the way out of its cave and was roaring mightily, lighting up the sky with its flaming breath.

Mother and I were watching the weather on television, the word MUTE in green in the top right corner of the screen. It was ten days before Christmas and the coast was getting drenched with another big thunderstorm, lots of rain and not much cold. She was sitting up in her bed, under the covers, and I was in an old rocker that was one of the few things she was using from my father's place. The rain outside sounded like a TV somebody had left on real loud after all the stations had gone off the air. Frank and Bosco were together in one corner of the room.

"You know, uh, there's something I need to tell you," she said.

"Oh yeah? What?"

"I don't think it's anything, but, well, I've been hearing voices," she said. She had her arms crossed over her chest, and once in a while she picked at her lip. "When I try to sleep I hear people breathing. They're very close to me, right next to me. I think it's your father, Ray. I should recognize his breathing, but I don't."

"C'mon, Mother," I said.

"It's him. I know it is."

"It's an auditory hallucination. Happens to the best of us." I rocked in the chair and switched channels, seeing if any other station had a camera out in the street. It really was a mess out there.

"It scares me," she said.

"I know. When he was over there alone, like after you moved, I used to think I heard him calling me in the middle of the night. You remember how he used to call me? 'Oh-Ray!' he'd call, like it was one word. I'd be trying to go to sleep and everything would be quiet and I'd hear that."

"Is that true?"

"Yeah," I said. "At first I thought it was some kind of supernatural communication, like he was in trouble and needed me. Like he was having a heart attack or something and just called out, and by some magic, at the same time hundreds of miles away, I heard it. A couple times I called over there just to be sure, but he was always fine. I still hear him sometimes, when the water is running in the bath, or the sink. I have to cut off the faucets to be sure it's nothing."

"I wish he had come," my mother said. "We could have had a good time over here. He was such a hardhead."

"He wasn't so bad," I said.

"No," she said. "He was fine. I miss him. I'm glad you're here, and Jewel and RV, but I miss your father. I was planning to spend my declining years with him."

"Well, you can decline with us now. How's that?"

"Oh, you're just kids," she said.

"Yeah, but we're planning a long, slow decline starting last week. Nothing abrupt. House rules. Maybe forty years. You got forty years left in you?"

My mother did a pirate face that I recognized instantly. It was a face she'd been making at me since I was a kid. "Why sure," she said.

Jewel called from work to say that she wanted to go out to eat. She wanted to know what Mother and RV were doing. I said my mother was resting in bed and RV was spending the night with Mallory, and I asked why she wanted to go out in the terrible weather.

My mother switched her forefinger back and forth to tell me she wasn't going anywhere. "I'm in for the night," she whispered.

"Chinese," Jewel said. "I'm coming to get you in a cab."

"Mom's stuck in bed and she can't get up," I said.

"Well, we'll bring her something," Jewel said. "What does she like that's Chinese? I'm getting a cab now."

"We'll bring you Chinese food?" I said to my mother, lifting the phone away from my mouth.

She shrugged.

"Fine," I said to Jewel. "I'm ready and waiting."

Half an hour later she called again, this time from a gas station about a mile up the highway. "It's great out here, Ray," she said. "The cabbie had to pull off because 90's flooding. Everybody's splashing around, and the guy running this place says there are snakes everywhere. I've seen two."

"You've seen snakes?"

"Yep. They look like tiny Loch Ness monsters," she said. "They float around in the water with their heads sticking out."

"Terrific," I said.

"The cabbie says he won't go anymore."

"Why don't I come get you?"

"That'd be great. This cab guy is a grease gun anyway."

"Sit tight. I'll be there in a flash." I hung up and thumbed the remote on the television, going through the channels looking for something about the flooding. The closest I got was a disheveled guy in shirtsleeves with his collar loosened and his tie pulled down, waving at a chroma-key map of the coast.

I tried to punch the button for sound, but I missed and I had to punch a couple of other buttons, and when I finally got the sound turned up, the station was in the middle of a bean commercial.

"Go, Ray," my mother said. "Give me the switcher."

I kissed her forehead and went to my room for a raincoat, then went out the side door and jumped into the big Oldsmobile. It was late afternoon. The sky was dark, veined in pinks and pale grays. Thunder cracked around. Lightning zigzagged like some maniac's lab. The rain came in clumps, spattering off the windshield, hammering the roof and hood. I backed out of the drive, got up in the center of Torch Street, riding high. All the yards in the neighborhood were glistening, all the grass was ankle-deep in water. The drainage ditches along the road were overflowing. A woman in a housedress was on a porch with a dog, both of them looking out a screen door. Most houses had their lights on inside. I saw people moving toward and away from windows. The brown horse was tied to its tree, shiny and clean.

I gave the Olds some gas, then eased back and let the big car roll. I didn't want to stir up a lot of water. I had the driver's window open, but the rain was slanting away, so the inside stayed pretty dry. The light had a greenish glow.

The wipers ratcheted back and forth, but I couldn't see much. A couple of blocks from the house a dog approached on the driver's side of the car and started walking with me, eyeing the front wheel as if to decide whether to bite the tire.

"What are you doing, bugs?" I said to the dog. "Why are you out in the rain?" The dog turned its head and kind of squinted at me, then went back to the tire. I gave the gas a squirt and the Olds jumped. The dog stopped dead, then trotted up again. "We're going for Chinese. Want to come?" I said. "Oh, wait. I guess not, now that I think about it."

The dog lifted its head and rolled its eyes back, looking at me almost upside down.

"You go on home now." I waved my arm at the dog, trying to get it to stop following.

Two kids were inside a refrigerator box, open end toward the street, on the lawn of a gray house. It looked as though they were playing soldiers.

The headlights reflected off the flying rain. I could barely see out front, it was a glittering hash of water blown sideways, splashing off the road. As I came out from under the oaks near the highway, things lightened up. The sky was gray-white. I could make out cars going by with their lights shining. People were idling along single file, trying to avoid the deep parts. I snapped on my blinker and waited for a burgundy Cadillac, a delivery van, and a modern car I didn't know the name of. When they'd passed I edged out into the street, made the left, and rode the crown of the highway.

A few cars were pulled off onto the concrete overlooking the beach, but traffic moved smoothly. At the gas station on the corner of Highway 90 and Fulmer, I found Jewel under the overhang, chewing a stick of red licorice. Three or four other people huddled by the Coke machine. Jewel got in and planted a kiss on the side of my mouth.

"Hello, mighty husband," she said.

I arched an eyebrow and swung the Olds back into the rain. She patted my thigh.

"We roll," she said.

"Where're we going?"

"Into the future," she said.

I got back on the beach highway. Cars were inching along, kicking up waves. The wipers swam across the glass. At Caroline Prince Road Jewel said, "Here we are."

"Oh yeah," I said, hitting my signal. The restaurant was

Shanghai Garden. The food wasn't great, but the place was never crowded and the people who ran it were friendly. The building had once been a convenience store. Inside, there was enameled latticework, green leatherette, a wall of mirrors, and a buffet table the restaurant never used. The windows had red burlap curtains. The rest was dark green with red trim and gold highlights. Here and there white lanterns with red tassels hung from the ceiling, and on the walls the usual dragons.

We got menus and took a booth by the window. The menus were stained. The tablecloth was dark green and stained, and the place mats were paper and printed with the Chinese zodiac.

"Are you a dog?" Jewel said. "I can't remember if you're a dog or a horse."

"Horse," I said.

"Look at that," she said. "We're perfectly suited for each other. See here?" She tapped the section on my place mat under the drawing of the horse. "I'm highly compatible with the horse."

"Are we eating?" I said.

At one end of the room there was a giant rear-screen projection television with a VCR sitting on top. It was showing some kind of Chinese talent show.

We ordered soup, pot stickers, house vegetables deluxe, and lemon chicken. I got up and swiped a fork from a table next to ours.

"Did RV tell you about Lake Forgetful?" I said.

"Sure did. She wants a mobile home, right? Not the way I imagined things."

"I wouldn't mind," I said. "We'd have to get one for Mother."

"I'm game if that's what you want to do," she said. "It has a certain appeal."

"It's strange out there," I said. "All the mailboxes are in this one row, but the trailers are cockeyed all over. It's hilly right there, and these trailers are tucked in at the feet of the pines, high and low, like discarded cocoons. She tell you about the guys we saw?"

"The pissers? Yes. She told me. Do you long to go down and pee in the lake of an evening?"

"I'd like to do it once before I die," I said.

"Yada yada," she said. "So here's this true story I heard today. Want to hear?"

"Sure," I said.

"Eve, the social worker, has a brain-damaged client who loves Hillary Clinton, so when Hillary is promoting her book in New Orleans the client wants to go. They're in line for a signed book, and the woman's fidgeting, so Eve tells her to think of a question to ask Mrs. Clinton. That calms the woman down. When they get to Hillary the woman falls on her knees and says, 'Mrs. President, thank you for everything you've done for mental health, and why does the Navy always make people retire early?' "

I laughed, then stopped laughing and looked at Jewel.

"I know," she said.

"Some things are so wonderful in this world," I said.

Jewel smoothed her place mat and rearranged her napkin, her water glass, her utensils. Then she started on the lazy Susan, where the sweet and sour sauces were, where the soy sauce was, where the chrome rack of Sweet & Low sat. When she got that policed, she started to work on my place setting. I pulled back the red burlap curtain and looked outside into the frizzy rain. Two police cars had pulled up and blocked the highway. Their lights were flashing and the policemen were out in bright yellow slickers directing traffic, detouring it off the beach highway. The glass rattled with faraway thunder.

Across the road a single mottled gray smear ran all the way from the beach up into the clouds. There was no horizon. The rain was relentless. The policemen were in it calf-deep. Cars plowed the water. The stoplight was blinking green.

The food came, and as we ate I listened to the music playing in the restaurant — a Chinese tune, one hundred sixty beats per minute at least. Chinese rock music. I watched Jewel cool her soup in the large white spoon. She was stunning, remarkable. I tapped my mouth with my napkin, then slid out of my side of the booth and got into hers. She was startled and pushed away.

"Shh," I said, holding up a hand. I reached out and touched her hair, ran my fingers through it, the tips of my fingers reaching to her scalp.

"What are you doing?" she said. "Get back over there."

"In a minute."

"Go on." She shooed me with her napkin. I pulled her to me. She resisted at first, but then, perhaps sensing that I wasn't going to give up, she relented and allowed herself closer, and I kissed her softly on the cheek and then on her neck beneath her ear. I let my head rest on her shoulder a minute, then kissed her there, sat up, and edged out of the booth. I stood for a minute, took a drink of Diet Coke, and stared across the room at the big television.

Jewel caught my hand, gave me a tug toward my seat.

I listened to the rain and to that strange music and felt Jewel's hand and thought of my mother's hand, the skin almost translucent now, and of RV, and of my dead father, and of everything that had happened to us, and I wondered why we always try to make things predictable, when it's clear that what happens will always be mysterious and peculiar.

I sat down in the booth.

I had no appetite, but put two or three things on my plate,

busied myself moving them back and forth, moving them clockwise. "How come you're not using chopsticks?"

"No need," she said.

"It makes a more complete experience," I said. "That's what you told me."

"Somebody must have told me once," she said.

I pulled back the curtain again. Outside, there were more flashing, glittering, blinking lights. There were new policemen and there was a wrecker and there was a truck that had somehow jackknifed off the low sea wall. There were even some pink burning torches — the kind that come in emergency road kits. I could hear the buzz of the blinking Shanghai Garden sign mounted inside the glass near the booth where we sat.

" 'You long to see the great pyramids of Egypt,' " I said. "That's the fortune I got the last time we were here."

"Do you?" she said.

"No," I said.

"So, do you want to know why I called?" Jewel said. The rain had let up, and we were walking around in the lot outside Eddie Pepper Acura on Highway 49, north of Gulfport, looking at used cars. There was a lot of swooshing going on as water ran off into the street drains. Eddie Pepper was asking top dollar for practically everything. We'd always gone car shopping at night. I was thinking maybe we could get a fancier used car, maybe an Acura, maybe an old BMW, something to make up for the loss of both Explorers.

"Sure I want to know," I said. "But meanwhile I think we ought to look in the paper and forget the lots."

"Why don't you ask Randy at the Ford place?" Jewel said.

"I called him. He doesn't have anything. He's got a white pickup. You want a white pickup? It's five years old. Low mileage, mint condition is what he told me."

"A truck?" Jewel said. "Sounds great. RV would like it. Air conditioning and everything? What's wrong with it?"

"It's a truck," I said.

"So?" Jewel said. "It's time for a truck."

"You haven't even seen it. We ought to at least see it."

So we climbed back in the Oldsmobile and headed for Highway 90, and then east toward Biloxi for a look at the Ford dealership.

"So here's why I called," Jewel said. She hauled her purse up between us on the seat. "I've got something here you'll be interested in." She was messing with the purse, digging around in it.

"What is it?" We stopped at a light. I twisted the bag trying to see what was inside.

"It's dynamite." She pulled out a stack of hundred-dollar bills as thick as a cigarette box. "Ka-boom!" she said, grinning. "We are back in the danger zone, on the red-hot wire high above the city of Biloxi, Mississippi, swaying in the wind. I say we stop at the Paradise and go for the big one." She reached across the seat and brushed my cheek with the money.

"Really?" I said.

"We go in, slap this down, tell the fool to deal. Play one hand for as much as we've got. Then we walk."

Shivers ran off my spine. I was grinning like an idiot. "You are crazy," I said. "Jewel. Didn't I just do this?"

"And look how well it worked out," she said.

"Yeah, but everything's O.K. now, do we really want to fuck with it? I thought you liked everything better."

"I do," she said. "I really do, but we've got to take a last shot, I mean, what's the point otherwise? You know? I've got six thousand dollars here. A couple hits and we're in business, we're right back where we started."

"Oh gee, thanks. That's just where I want to be," I said.

"It's a figure of speech," she said. "We're here now, that other thing is finished. So if we go to the Paradise now, it's different. We're other people."

I felt like somebody had stuck a shunt in my side and was shoveling in the adrenaline. My heart was hammering. Another shot at it. That's what I'd been thinking about. It was hard not to shake.

The Paradise was in front of us soon enough. I steered the Olds into the casino lot. There were spaces everywhere. I parked right in front of the main entrance. None of this garage shit. We weren't going to be there that long. We were going to hit 'em hard and get out fast. Jewel took my hand in the front seat. The windshield was still covered with water drops that caught and curved the violet- and lime-colored light. I had a jumpy stomach.

"Fuck 'em," I said.

"You ready?" she said. "This is so not right. It couldn't be better."

We got out of the car and walked hand in hand across the lot and into the front door of the Paradise. It was still jangling in there, but the noise was sparer than I remembered. I didn't recognize anybody, they were all day-shift people. We crossed the goofy floor and stopped in the blackjack salon. There were four dealers, three of them standing behind fanned decks. The fourth was dealing to a black guy who looked like a sports star or something. He had a giant diamond ring on one of his fingers. I tried to see what it was, but couldn't.

"You like any of these?" Jewel said.

"You pick," I said. "It's your show."

"What, you're not in this?"

"Up to here," I said.

By midnight the rain was back, a foggy drizzle that settled on the town like cheap icing. At the Ford dealer the truck Randy was talking about was parked out on the corner, raked at a big angle, glowing in the bright lights of the lot. The glass was bubbled and the paint was beaded, and there were slurry paw prints where a cat had passed through. Jewel smeared away a spot on the window and pressed her face to the glass like a kid looking into a toy store.

"It kills me," she said. "It's perfect. Can you see us in a pickup? No, I mean it. This is it. It couldn't be more right."

"It's sort of utilitarian," I said.

"It's delivery boy," she said. "It's one hundred percent delivery boy."

We got back into my mother's car, but Jewel didn't want to leave, she wanted to sit and look at the pickup. "This is it. Like a sign of our new start."

"We're starting slow," I said.

"Yeah, well," she said. "Who cares?" She rolled down her window four or five inches, letting in fresh, wet air, then fumbled in her purse for a cigarette.

"You're smoking again?" I said.

"Very occasionally," she said. "To remind myself what it's like. I was bumming them off folks at the casino." She lit the cigarette and blew the smoke at the slot where the window was open.

"We could have just slid right on by," I said.

"Yeah, but you go downtown, you gotta dance," she said. "I don't know why I don't feel bad, but I don't. I feel great. I wish we'd done this years ago."

"You are a blessing," I said. "If we were sitting here with nails in our faces, you'd find something to like about it."

"What else can you do?" We listened to the almost inaudible rain for a few minutes. "I'm tired of worrying. We were trained to worry, to anticipate, to imagine. I'm telling you, RV's doing better than I was at her age. She's Saint Teresa the Little Flower compared to me."

"I dreamed of her last night," I said.

"Saint Teresa?"

I laughed and raised my chin at the windshield. "You really want this?"

"And all that goes with it," Jewel said. "We're going to be riding high. We're going to be real. We're going to take our lumps and not even notice. We're going to haul shit around in the back of that thing. We're going to drive down the street with Frank back there. His nails clicking on the metal. His face out in the wind, biting at it. The wind blowing his jaws open, blowing his dewlaps."

"What are dewlaps?" I said.

"I don't know. Something under here," she said, motioning under her chin.

"Frank's great," I said.

"We're all great," Jewel said. "That's what I'm trying to tell you here. Except for the knickknacks, they missed us. We won. They didn't lay a glove on us. We just had to clean out that little bit that was left over, and now we're set."

The windshield of my mother's car was hazy, dotted with knots of rain. The dashboard was lit with drippy-looking shadows cast by the tall lights in the used car lot. Occasionally a pair of headlights with a car attached went by out in the street. I liked sitting in the lot, hidden among all those used cars and trucks. I liked the stillness of it. Maybe that was what I liked, that stillness. I watched the silver and yellow aluminum streamers rattle and shake as the wind caught them. The lights from the used car lot and from the places across the street smeared in the hazy glass. I forearmed the window on the driver's side and the big lights outside turned into star-shaped tracers. Shorter, more intense. A gold light on top of a building across the street was perfectly biblical. Every light was doing a different thing, looked different in the glass. Some multiplied into fireworks, some had wings, some hung on the sides of buildings, barely glowing. A light out Jewel's side of the windshield grew and changed like a green lava lamp as the rain ran down the glass.

The stoplight changed and a mini-truck rolled by with its speakers cranked, pumping out the bass. Underneath, this truck was lined with violet neon that reflected on the wet street, making a pool of light to travel in, wonderful and otherworldly.

"There we go tomorrow," Jewel said. "The music and the light."

"You must be right," I said.

Jewel curled up in the seat, her back against the door. Outside the passenger glass a black panel van was parked at the end of a row of vans. I thought we ought to line up the Oldsmobile, preserve the order of things, so I started the engine and backed around to get us into place. It took a couple of tries, twisting the wheel, pulling us in close, but not too close, and perfectly parallel with the van, the old tires crackling on the blacktop, but when we were on target I ran down all the windows and cut the engine. We listened to a freight train hustle by, its whistle blaring, its wheels checking the tracks. We could hear the freight for a long time after it was gone, way off in the distance, and then when we couldn't hear it anymore we just sat there listening to this rain come out of the night. There was no end to it.